SWEET PROMISE

Sweet Promise

by

Juliet Gray

Dales Large Print Books
Long Preston, North Yorkshire,
BD23 4ND, England.

British Library Cataloguing in Publication Data.

Gray, Juliet
    Sweet Promise.

    A catalogue record of this book is
    available from the British Library

    ISBN   1-84262-189-0 pbk

First published in Great Britain in 1962 by
Wright & Brown Ltd.

Copyright © 1962 Juliet Gray

Cover illustration © Ben Turner by arrangement with
P.W.A. International

The moral right of the author has been asserted

Published in Large Print 2002 by arrangement with
Juliet Burton Literary Agency

Dales Large Print is an imprint of Library Magna Books Ltd.

Printed and bound in Great Britain by
T.J. (International) Ltd., Cornwall, PL28 8RW

CHAPTER ONE

It was an imposing house situated high on a hill overlooking the village and the surrounding countryside. It was more than a house. It was a mansion, built on sweeping, elegant lines and set in its own vast grounds. A long, wide drive leading from heavily-wrought gates set in a creeper-covered wall which surrounded the estate swept up to the house with its long stone terrace, wide stone steps and marble colonnades which gave every appearance of the mansions of the Deep South of America – and this was exactly what the owner had intended. Rolling lawns, gay profusion of flower beds, red-roofed stables beyond which were two verdant pastures for grazing, acres of wild land and a dark, intriguing copse reached by crossing a small stone bridge over a whispering stream – all these things emphasised the wealth of Stephen Power, who was the richest man in the county. The villagers said that he was the richest man in England but that was an exaggeration. Certainly he had more money than he could possibly use in his lifetime but his sons made great inroads into that income.

Stephen Power was a small, burly man with an indefinable magnetism and a sense of his own importance. He had been born in the slums of a big industrial town and his childhood had been miserable, hunger-ridden and brief. To Stephen, it had been bearable only because of his dreams of the future. A lonely boy, he had spoken of them to no one – but with an inborn deter-mination he had converted them from dreams to reality.

Now, the many grand edifices – office buildings, factories, hotels and blocks of luxury flats – were all tributes to his name. Power Constructions Ltd. were known all over the world and his early background was forgotten to all but Stephen. Even his wife, who had died in childbirth, had never known that he was the son of an out-of-work Irish labourer and a kitchen-maid.

He enjoyed his wealth to the utmost. Nothing was beyond his means and he denied his children nothing that they demanded. He had loved his wife and he never married again – content with the hours he spent in his offices and touring the construction sites, content in his home and his family.

He was not a popular man but that caused him no anxiety. His blunt manner often amounted to downright rudeness: his opinions covered a variety of subjects and were too often impressed upon others as the only right and sensible way of thinking; he did not tolerate fools gladly and trusted no one, not even his closest friends. He could afford to laugh anyone in the face and frequently did. He went his own way without heed for advice, opinion or opposition.

On a warm evening in June, when the sunset streaked the sky with red and gold, he stood on the stone terrace, overlooking the garden, his firm, strong hands resting lightly on the balustrade. His leonine head thrown back, shouting with laughter which echoed throughout the big house, he bawled encouragement to his two oldest sons who were engaged in a wrestling match despite the fact that each was mounted on a powerful stallion. The restive horses tore up the ground beneath their feet, whinnying shrilly. The brothers were grunting with the strain, each determined not to give in, each determined that the other would be dislodged from his seat. They were evenly matched and Stephen was delighted with the contest, shouting encouragement to each in turn, criticising and condemning, approving and advising as he watched.

He heard a soft footstep behind him and turned as his youngest son approached. For a moment, his eyes narrowed scornfully – then he clapped his heavy hand on the boy's shoulder. 'Well, Jonothan! Come to see the fun? I'll stake a hundred on Adam – what do you say?'

Jonothan Power, slim and pale, his sensitive features a striking contrast to the ruddy heartiness and faint grossness of his father's face, looked briefly at his brothers and then he turned away. 'Isn't it time you changed for the evening, Father? It's getting late.'

Stephen glanced at the gold watch with its wide band that he wore on his wrist. 'Time enough, boy. I want to see this – I'm damned if Russ isn't tiring. But he has the courage of a lion – just like his old man, eh, Jonothan?' His eyes glistened with pride. 'Look at those shoulders – like a young bull! The powerful Powers! No wonder the villagers say it with awe. I'd be sorry for any of the village lads that Russ took on in a fight.'

'So you should be, Father,' Jonothan

retorted sternly. 'He broke Jacob Flint's jaw last week.'

'So I heard – so I heard. He's a great boy with his fists. Pity we can't put him in the ring. He'd be a champion inside six months.'

Jonothan looked long at his father – then with a brief sigh he turned to watch his brothers. With one mighty heave, Adam seized his brother about the waist and threw him from the saddle to the ground. Russ lay prone for a moment then he rolled over and got to his feet, grinning broadly. He caught the reins and remounted in a leap – then waved gaily to Stephen before leaning across to whack Adam's horse hard on the rump. The horse, startled, bolted and it took all of Adam's time to control him for the reins had lain slackly across his neck while he sat laughing at his brother and he was nearly thrown when the horse reared.

As the two brothers galloped away, Stephen turned from the balustrade – and his gaze fell once more on his youngest son. It had been a bitter blow to him that this boy had cost his wife's life. It had been harder still for him to accept the truth that Jonothan would be a weakling all his life for a foot had been injured during his birth and he was slightly lame. He had never been

interested in the games and pranks under-
taken by his brothers even if he had been
able to join in them. He was a great reader
and student and Stephen was often baffled
by the boy, although he was justifiably
proud of his brains. To Stephen, it was a
personal blow to his pride that he had
fathered a son like Jonothan who was so
very different to the other boys.

He was kind but often impatient with
Jonothan. It did not improve matters when
he occasionally realised, despite his lack of
insight, that Jonothan disapproved of him
and sought to reprove him with his quiet
speech and air of dignified composure and
his love of books. Stephen had no time for
books unless they dealt with finance and he
could not understand that Jonothan could
read and enjoy the classics and spend hours
in his room studying.

Now he stood looking critically at the boy.
He was already dressed for the evening in a
black dinner suit and spotless, starched
linen, his deep bronze hair neatly brushed.
He was tall, as his mother had been, but
slight with small hands and feet. Stephen
often declared that a good puff of wind
would knock the boy over, implying his
pride in the height, breadth and strength of

his other sons.

'Dressed to kill, eh? For the Armstrong girl's benefit, I suppose.' He snorted.

Jonothan flushed painfully. 'For your benefit, Father.'

Stephen grunted. 'I can believe that, eh? Do you take me for a fool?' He did not wait for an answer but strode into the house, Jonothan following him. 'Pour me a drink, boy.' Jonothan crossed to the decanters and poured a stiff tot of whiskey into a glass which he handed to his father. 'I shall look a fine figure dolled up for the occasion, won't I?' Stephen went on. 'Oh well, we don't throw a party for your sister every day of the week, do we?' He hated formal clothes, happiest when he could stride around in rough tweeds or comfortable, shabby trousers with a brightly coloured shirt. He threw himself into a chair, stared long and hard at the amber whiskey and said quietly: 'You're wasting your time with that chit – you know that, I suppose?' He had a habit of turning his remarks into questions but seldom expected answers. 'She's pretty enough, I know – but I hope for a better match than that for you, Jonothan.'

'I'm in love with Nancy,' Jonothan said quietly.

Stephen stared at him then roared with laughter. 'Love! What does a boy of twenty know of love? But I should have expected such stupid talk from you, shouldn't I? My son in love with a vicar's daughter! Oh, I'm not saying anything against the girl or her father, understand that. But you can do better for yourself than choose a girl without any income or decent background. God knows your brothers bring enough of the right kind of girls to the house. Why can't you fancy yourself in love with one of them, eh?'

The colour stained Jonothan's cheeks and his lips tightened with anger. But he knew better than to attempt argument with his father. His voice was very quiet but firm as he replied: 'I'm sorry, Father. But I want to marry Nancy. Money doesn't mean very much to either of us...'

Stephen did not let him continue. 'Easy to talk like that when you have plenty, eh, Jonothan? The girl's no fool – not that I believe she's interested in your money. Oddly enough, she seems to understand you which is more than I can claim, isn't it? Don't look so grim, boy. I've no intention of cutting you off without a penny. Marry the girl – it doesn't matter to me.'

16

'I intend to marry her.'

Stephen looked at him sharply, caught by the quiet decision in his son's voice. He studied him intently, noting the determination in the line of his jaw and in his grey eyes, observing the set of the slight shoulders. 'So you do, do you? Without my blessing or with it, I suppose?'

'I shall be twenty-one in December,' Jonothan reminded him. 'Nancy's father hasn't any objection so we plan to marry in the Spring. I know it doesn't really matter to you whom I marry – but both Nancy and I would prefer to marry with your blessing.'

'Heavens, boy, do as you like! Have I ever stopped any of you from doing what you want to do?' He tossed the whiskey neatly to the back of his throat, set the glass sharply on the table and rose to his feet. 'I'm going to change. As you're ready you can hold the fort if anyone arrives before I'm down.' He smiled kindly at Jonothan. 'I've no objection to Nancy, my son. She's your kind of woman – but I'm hoping your brothers will have more sense when they marry!'

He strode from the room with his heavy tread, a powerful man in his late fifties, radiating health and strength and force. Jonothan toyed idly with his father's empty glass and thought of their recent exchange with a vague restlessness...

In a large room in the upper part of the house, a girl sat before the mirror of her dressing-table while her maid brushed her long, auburn hair. The room was feminine and elegantly furnished in soft shades of lilac and silver. She hummed softly to herself, turning her head this way and that to study the effect, regardless of the maid's efforts to brush the silken tresses which gleamed in the soft lights.

On the wide bed behind her lay a white evening dress – a cascade of filmy organza and tulle which she was to wear that night. Suddenly she rose from the stool and walked over to the open windows. The curtains billowed in the soft, summery breeze and she stood gazing at the sunset, raising her hands to lift the cloud of hair from her bare, creamy shoulders.

'Someone might see you, Miss Promise. Do come away from the window,' urged the maid anxiously. 'The guests will be arriving any minute now.'

The girl turned with a light laugh. 'I'm not worried, Estelle. I'm not ashamed of my body.' She looked down at herself – slim, curvaceous body in its brief silken coverings

– and then turned to survey herself in the long wall mirror. 'No, I'm not ashamed of my body,' she repeated.

'Do let me finish your hair,' the maid urged again. 'You'll be late.'

'I mean to be. I shall make a grand entrance,' Promise told her lightly. She was a beautiful girl: her sweeping mass of auburn hair framed a bewitchingly lovely face with its wide-spaced grey eyes, small, straight nose and wide, curving mouth with its natural rich colour. She moved nearer to the mirror and looked anxiously at her nose. 'Damn! Look at these freckles, Estelle! I hate freckles – they're so girlish!'

'I warned you about the sun – you wouldn't wear a hat and you laughed when I told you the freckles would come out.'

'Oh, I don't care! A few freckles won't spoil my looks, will they?' She went back to the dressing-table. 'Do my hair quickly, Estelle. I don't want to be so late that I miss anything.'

Promise Power had been born two years before Jonothan. Her unusual name had been bestowed upon her by her mother. After the birth of three sons, when she had learned that she was expecting another child, she had hugged Stephen and said lightly: 'This one will be a girl – and that's a promise!' During the months of pregnancy, they had always spoken of the expected baby as the 'promise' and when she was born, Stephen had insisted upon naming her Promise and his wife had laughingly concurred although she warned him that no one would ever believe it was the child's name. Her looks and the name combined had sufficed to attract second glances all through her life and Promise had no complaint to make about her unusual name. She enjoyed the fine-sounding announcement of 'Promise Power'. But Promise enjoyed everything in life, particularly the amusing pastime of twisting her father around her little finger, for, although he loved and prided his sons, she was his favourite.

Swiftly and skilfully, the maid twisted Promise's lovely hair into a smooth and gleaming chignon at the back of her proud head and then helped her mistress into the following white dress which emphasised her creamy complexion and clung to the curves of her body as though it had been moulded to her. Bare, creamy shoulders rose smoothly from the pleated folds of the gown and the provocative swelling of her young breasts

20

above the bodice caused the maid to exclaim. Promise studied herself. 'Perhaps it is a little low,' she admitted. Suddenly she pulled a white rose from the bowl on the table, snapped off its long stem and tucked the beautiful head between her breasts 'There!' she exclaimed. 'That looks better.'

Estelle sniffed. 'It will soon die. Flowers always fade on flirts, Miss Promise.'

Promise opened her eyes in wide innocence. 'Oh, Estelle, I'm not a flirt!'

'No, miss – I know it doesn't seem like it,' she returned stolidly and with a trace of country accent, for her real name was Esther and Promise had bestowed the French name upon her, 'but you don't deceive me even if the men think that butter wouldn't melt in your mouth!'

Promise laughed. 'Oh, you know too much, my good Estelle! And you don't really approve of me! But I don't care. I'm my father's daughter and I care for nobody, no, not I, but everyone cares for me,' she misquoted mischievously.

Just as she spoke, there was a scuffle of steps outside the room, a murmur of angry voices and a thud against the door. Promise flew to the door and opened it swiftly. Fiery-haired Adam was standing, fists clenched, glowering at his brother Brent who was just picking himself up from the thickly-carpeted floor, cursing volubly and crudely, a red mark on his cheek where Adam's knuckles had caught him.

Promise laughed. 'Fighting again? Can't you two agree for one night?'

Brent threw her an angry glance. 'Don't interfere! This is strictly between Adam and I!' He turned and squared up to Adam with raised fists.

Swiftly Promise thrust herself between the two men. 'I won't have it!' she cried. 'Not tonight. If you must fight save it for tomorrow. I'm not having either of you appear with a black eye or a cut lip tonight!' She stamped her foot angrily.

The sign of her tempestuous anger caused both brothers to burst out laughing. Then they grinned at each other. 'Okay,' Adam said. 'I'll let you off tonight. But keep your foul tongue to yourself in future.'

Brent turned to Promise. 'I only said that Julie Wentworth is easy game for any man. You agree with me, don't you, Promise?'

The angry colour mounted to Adam's face and he stepped forward again, swinging his fist up to his brother's chin. Brent moved back quickly and the blow missed but the heavy ring which Adam wore on his little finger caught his lip and split it. A dark bead of blood welled up.

'Oh, of course she is!' Promise cried. 'Everyone knows that. Adam, don't be a fool!'

Attracted by the rumpus, a door opened further down the hall and Stephen stepped out, dressed only in dark evening trousers, his powerful chest bare but for mass of red hair. 'What the hell…!' he bawled. Then he grunted with understanding. 'Must you make so much noise?' he asked mildly as he came up to them. He caught Brent's face between his strong fingers and examined the swiftly-darkening bruise on his cheek and the bleeding lip. 'Put some arnica on that bruise,' he commanded. 'Go and clean yourself up, you big lout.' He turned to Adam. 'That's enough. You'll both behave yourselves tonight. Nothing is going to spoil this party for Promise – understand!'

The brothers were no match for their father's anger or the deadly impact of his fist which they had known more than once so they looked at each other, shrugged and then dropped their fighting stances. Brent turned away and went back to his room as the heavy bell pealed downstairs and the firm tread of Mathieson was heard as he went to answer the door. Stephen slipped his arm about Promise's shoulders. 'You look beautiful, my girl,' he said indulgently.

She laughed into his heavy face so close to her own. 'You don't, Father. Go and get dressed, for heaven's sake. The Freemans have arrived.' She turned to Adam. 'Will you take me down, Adam?'

'Yes, take your sister down,' approved Stephen. 'I meant to do it myself but I can't go down like this.' He gave his eldest son a quick once-over. 'Yes, you'll do.' He grinned proudly. 'Trust you not to get marked in a fight, my son.'

Adam shrugged. 'Are you ready, Promise?' He ignored his father's words.

'Yes – oh no, I haven't any shoes on!' Her musical laugh fluted through the house and the guests below, busily divesting themselves of stoles and gloves and what-have-you, looked upwards and then murmured to each other. Promise darted into her room, thrust aside the helpful Estelle and slipped on the white, high-heeled evening shoes.

She paused for a moment at the head of the stairs, looking up at Adam with a smile in her eyes. 'Well, what do you think?'

'You're adorable, you bewitching brat!' he

told her with a grin. 'And you know it!'

She tossed her head. Then, assuming a demure air, she slipped her hand in his arm and walked with him down the wide, sweeping staircase, smiling sweetly and almost shyly upon the newly-arrived guests.

CHAPTER TWO

The hired orchestra swung into a medley of popular tunes and within a few moments the highly-polished floor of the ballroom was occupied by dancing couples.

Stephen Power stood in the doorway, surveying the colourful and lively scene with more than a little satisfaction. His keen grey eyes sought his daughter and he espied her dancing with Russ and he nodded approval. She had never been a girl to thrust herself too eagerly upon men other than her brothers and although she was much-admired, no one could call her a flirt. This pleased him very much for he was blind to the fact that it was an amusing pretence which gave Promise a great deal of secret amusement and pleasure. It was early in the evening yet but it would not be long before she was dancing with other men.

Adam passed him as he stood there, an attractive, dark-haired girl with mocking eyes for his partner. He whirled her about the room with expert ease, an excellent dancer and an extremely handsome man with his fiery hair, tall, broad physique and swift, brilliant smile.

Brent was not in the ballroom and a tiny frown creased Stephen's forehead for he knew instinctively that his son would be in the small room adjoining which served as a bar on these occasions. He hoped that Brent would not drink too much as he usually did. He hoped too that the boys would remember his warning and curb their quick tempers. He wanted no fighting at this party which was being held to celebrate Promise's twenty-third birthday.

He looked around for Jonothan and his lips twisted with a trace of contempt as he noticed the boy. He was standing by one of the tall marble pillars talking to a young, sweet-faced girl in a pale blue dress and Stephen recognised Nancy Armstrong. They were well-matched, he told himself with a snort. A wishy-washy pair with no lust for life, preferring books and quiet walks and the peaceful tenor of an existence which held no thrills, no drama, no excitement.

Richard Wentworth nodded to him affably and Stephen grinned. The man was always affable and so he should be considering how deeply in debt he was to Stephen Power. He strode across to him.

'Evening, Richard. Not drinking? Come and have one with me, will you?'

The man fell into step beside him and they went across the ballroom and entered the bar. As Stephen had anticipated, Brent was standing by it, a glass in his hand, his grey eyes glowering darkly. The mark on his cheek was still noticeable and a tiny drop of dark blood still marred his lower lip. Richard Wentworth greeted him with a nod.

Stephen obtained two drinks and handed one of them to his companion. 'Glad you could come,' he said abruptly.

'We never miss your parties,' Richard said lightly. 'Anne always enjoys herself and Julie is devoted to your boys.' He jerked his head in the direction of Brent. 'He looks as though he's been in trouble again. You have a difficult time of it with your sons.'

Stephen glared. 'Do you think so? I can handle them well enough.'

Richard hastily changed the subject. 'Promise looks very lovely tonight. You'll soon be losing her, I think – or so Anne tells me. She says that no father can hope to keep a lovely girl like Promise indefinitely.'

Stephen frowned. 'She hasn't any plans for

marriage to my knowledge. I'm in no hurry to lose her and she's in no hurry to go. She has everything she wants – why should she give it all up for some worthless man?'

Richard laughed. 'Oh, one day she'll consider the world well lost for love! You're fortunate that she hasn't rushed into marriage already. Plenty of men willing to marry a girl like Promise, I'll wager! What is she now? Twenty-three, is it?'

'Yes – and she still can't find any man as good as her father!' he boasted proudly.

Richard Wentworth murmured some polite reply but he privately considered such an attachment between father and daughter not only unhealthy but slightly ridiculous. He was quite fond of his own daughter but he had no illusions about her and it would be a relief when she decided to marry.

Stephen turned to him with some question about the market and the two men fell into an absorbing and lengthy discussion of stocks and shares...

Brent studied them with cynical eyes, his glass never empty for long. He could not hear their conversation but he had a shrewd conception of their discussion and he kept a discreet distance so that he should not be drawn into it. He was bored and slightly resentful that his evening should be wasted with such trivial entertainment. He was still annoyed with Adam who never pulled his punches with anyone, least of all with his brothers. He knew that he had spoken too carelessly of Julie Wentworth but he did not regret the truthful comment. He was amused by Adam's obvious interest in the girl – an interest which would quickly fade once he had proved for himself that she was easy game as Brent had claimed.

The Powers were universally disliked and resented in the district. They were reckless and devil-may-care, quick with their tongues and their fists, careless of the opinion of anyone but themselves, fond of women and contemptuous of those who did not appreciate their outlook on life. Their policy was to enjoy life to the utmost, damn the expense and their reputations, and who cared if their particular forms of enjoyment led to trouble or brushes with the law. Adam, Brent and Russ were all handsome and men of magnificent physique, superficially alike in looks and bearing but each with their own distinction.

Fast cars, fast horses and a fast whirl of social excitements were important to each of them. They drove their cars at full speed through quiet lanes, sleepy villages or busy towns. They urged their horses to a gallop over the moors which edged their father's land, leaping high hedges, streams and fences without a thought for their necks, trespassing without care on property that belonged to the farmers in the district. They spent a lot of time in London and were much amused when their various exploits reached the newspapers. They spent money like water – and they were all experts in this particular field, assisted by the knowledge that their father had no objection to their extravagance and loved to listen to their eyebrow-raising tales of the life they led.

Jonothan limped into the room and approached the bar. Brent moved to one side for him and while Jonothan waited for the drinks he ordered, the two brothers exchanged remarks.

'Why are you on your own?' Jonothan asked, with some surprise. He looked keenly at his brother's lip. 'Whose fist did you walk into?' he asked with a slight smile.

'Adam's,' Brent replied curtly. 'I'm on my own, dear Jonothan, because I prefer it that way.' He tossed off the contents of his glass.

Jonothan watched him but knew better than to comment on Brent's capacity for drink. 'Why do you stay if you're not enjoying yourself?'

'Express orders from the old man,' Brent retorted. He fingered his cut lip thoughtfully. 'He'll be sorry by the end of the evening.'

'Why?'

Brent grinned. 'Because I intend to return the compliment when I get a chance of riling Adam.'

Jonothan shrugged. 'What's the point?'

Brent glanced at him. Then he laughed. 'You mean that I'll get the worst of it?'

'Possibly.'

'Probably, in fact. But I'm in the mood to flex my fists a little.' He raised a hand and clenched it, studying it thoughtfully.

'It would be a pity to spoil the party for Promise,' Jonothan said quietly, knowing that Brent was devoted to his sister and might think twice if he was reminded how much she had looked forward to this party.

'Mm – that's true,' Brent conceded. 'Oh well, I won't pick on Adam in the house. I'll get him outside.' He grinned in pleased anticipation.

Jonothan said nothing. It always puzzled him that his brothers could be such good friends and yet enjoy fighting each other so much. He was no coward and there was nothing effeminate in his make-up but he viewed the fighting of brothers as distasteful and unnecessary.

He took the glasses and with a nod to his brother, went back to Nancy Armstrong who greeted him with a warm smile. 'Sorry I've been so long,' he said quietly. 'I was talking to Brent.'

'Oh, is he here?' Her eyes brightened but Jonothan did not notice that sudden gleam. 'I haven't seen him. I thought he'd decided not to bother with this party.'

'He's here – in the bar as usual.' Jonothan spoke grimly.

'I wonder why he drinks so much,' Nancy said softly.

Jonothan shrugged. 'Because he likes it, I guess.' He smiled at her. 'Don't worry about Brent. He can take care of himself, you know. Come and dance, Nancy.' He was not a good dancer although he persevered despite his lame foot. But Nancy slipped into his arms willingly and they merged with the group of dancers...

Promise, standing with Russ and a few of their friends, watched as Nancy and Jono-than went by. She turned to Russ. 'Look at that whey-faced little madam with Jon.

She's really bewitched him. Why can't he see that she doesn't give two hoots for him?'

Russ grinned. 'Why should you worry? Let him make a fool of himself if he wants. I don't approve his taste myself but I make a point of not interfering in other people's affairs!'

Promise frowned. 'She may be the vicar's daughter but there's nothing Christian about her interest in Jon.' Her eyes were scornful as she went on: 'I can't understand why she didn't concentrate on Adam from the beginning. She's not the type to be content with the youngest son's share of the estate when the old man moves on to a higher sphere.'

'Perhaps you're misjudging the girl,' Russ suggested. 'Anyway, is she Adam's type? Be your age, Promise.'

Promise scanned the girl from head to foot as she passed once more. 'No, she isn't,' she admitted. 'Adam likes his women to be gay and exciting and with ample curves in the right place. Nancy Armstrong would bore him to tears.'

'She bores me to tears too,' Russ cut in. 'Can't you talk of someone else?' He turned away to talk to his friends.

Her attention was caught by the steady

gaze of a man who stood a few feet away. Resenting his scrutiny, she did not return the smile he gave her and she turned her shoulder on him although she carefully maintained her expression of sweet demurity and modesty. She had long since discovered that such an approach attracted the men and kept them attracted whereas a girl like Julie Wentworth, undeniably attractive with her dark hair and bold, mocking eyes and lovely figure, failed to hold any man for any length of time.

A few minutes later, she glanced covertly towards him and felt swift annoyance as their eyes met and he laughed at her lack of resistance to his disturbing gaze. She tugged at her brother's arm. 'Russ, who is that man? By the pillar over there?'

Russ looked at him briefly. 'Damned if I know. Go and ask him,' he said and then turned back to the girl by his side.

Promise ignored his suggestion and tried to ignore the man. She accepted an invitation to dance and went on to the floor with her partner but while she was whirled about the room in his arms she was still conscious of the man's eyes upon her. Her temper began to rise. She knew very well that she had only to tell Adam or Brent that the man was annoying her and they would deal with him summarily – but she hesitated. She, like her father, wanted no trouble at this party and both Adam and Brent were too quick to start a fracas.

Her partner came to an abrupt stop as the man brushed past several couples to their side and tapped his shoulder. 'The lady feels like a change,' he said and before either Promise or her partner could object he had taken her into his arms and whirled her into the dance.

She disliked and yet admired the strength of his close embrace. She pulled back and looked up into his dark, lean face and then hastily looked away as she met his mocking eyes which disarmed her so completely.

'Don't you think that was a little high-handed?' she demanded haughtily.

His arm tightened about her waist. 'Agreed. But it's the quickest way to get what I want – and I wanted to dance with you. Any objection?'

'You're holding me too tightly – that's the first objection,' she told him coldly.

He laughed. 'I won't believe that worries you.'

'Well, it does.' She tried to ease his strong embrace and obligingly he released her slightly. 'Thank you,' she said in a tone like ice.

'What about your other objections?' he asked her mockingly.

The music stopped at that moment and she was saved a reply. She moved away from him. 'Please excuse me. I must go back to my friends,' she said smoothly, with emphasis on the last word.

'Come and have a drink with me,' he said and taking her arm in a vice-like grip he steered her towards the bar. 'Then you can call me one of your friends.'

Furious but helpless, Promise had no choice but to accompany him. She was even more tempted to call her brothers to her assistance but one glance about the crowded ballroom immediately changed her mind. With as good a grace as she could muster, she walked with him and en-deavoured to convey by her expression that she was perfectly willing to do so, despite that obvious grip on her arm and his forceful manner.

As they entered the bar-room, she threw a swift, appealing glance towards Brent but he looked at them without interest and turned towards the bar to have his glass refilled.

She almost spat the words at her companion. 'Do you know who I am?'

He shook his head. 'No, but I intend to find out. I've been watching you all evening – a very pleasant occupation, I might add. Do you know that you're a very lovely woman?'

The blaze of her eyes should have shrivelled him but he seemed completely unperturbed by the look she gave him. 'I'm Promise Power,' she said haughtily and waited for the usual impression which her name caused on people who had never met her but had naturally enough heard of the Powers.

He nodded. 'So this is your birthday party. Many happy returns, Promise Power. Tell me, where on earth did your parents dig up a name like that?'

She coloured angrily. 'What's wrong with my name?'

'Nothing, I suppose.' He caught the barman's eye. 'What are you drinking?'

'Whis...' Swiftly she changed her mind. 'Sherry, please.'

He grinned. 'Why don't you have a whiskey and enjoy yourself?'

'Sherry, please,' she said again, more firmly.

'Please yourself.' He obtained the drinks

and handed the glass of sherry to her. 'Here's to happiness – and may you have many more birthdays!' he said lightly.

Promise sipped her drink and then flashed him a look of contempt as the fiery whiskey burned the back of her throat.

Before she could speak, he said easily: 'Yes, I know it's whiskey. Fire to match fire. By the way my name's Nellin – Matthew Nellin. My friends call me Matt.' He glanced at her frigid face. 'You've not heard of me? Too bad of your old man.'

'You know my father?' There was disbelief in her tone and in her eyes.

'I should do. I work for him – and you needn't look down your nose,' he added abruptly as her face changed. 'I'm a first-class designer and your old man is no fool. I did all the blueprints for the latest project – Kennedy House.' He mentioned a vast block of modern offices which the Power Construction Company had recently erected in the heart of London's big city. Now Promise looked at him with interest. She had been impressed by the edifice and she had told her father that it was about time he employed a modern minded and brilliant designer for his projects. Now she was face to face with the man who had designed

Kennedy House and she could not help a vague admiration for his brilliance and foresight.

'Then I should have heard of you,' she said slowly. She wrinkled her brow in the effort to remember. Then she shook her head. 'I'm sorry but your name means nothing to me.'

He shrugged. 'You won't forget it, though,' he said briefly. He looked about him. 'This house is a marvel,' he said. 'I never thought I'd find anything like this outside the States.'

Her eyes brightened with interest. 'You're an American.'

He laughed. 'Don't let the accent fool you. I'm a Canadian. But I did most of my studying in the States. I met your father when he went to Ottawa to supervise the construction of Kilkenny Dam last year. I managed to convince him that the Power Construction Company needed a man like me on its pay-roll. I guess he doesn't regret it.'

She looked down at the glass in her hand. 'Did my father invite you tonight?'

He nodded. 'I'm not a gate-crasher. Of course he invited me. Said he'd be glad to have me meet his family. Somehow I expected you all to be kids. But some fellow told me that none of you are kids either in age or experience.'

She was intrigued. She had the impression that Matt Nellin was yet another who cared nothing for the opinion of others. His slow drawl was fascinating and he was undeniably handsome even if she disliked his forceful manner and his apparent unconcern for her coldness towards him.

'I'd like to see more of this house,' he went on. 'Couldn't you show me over it?'

'Now?' she asked in surprise.

'No time like the present.'

'But I can't leave the party,' she protested.

'You won't be missed for a few minutes,' he assured her.

'I'm afraid it's impossible,' she began as her father came into the room, caught sight of his daughter and the young designer he employed and admired so much, and came over to join them.

'I wondered if you'd turn up, Matt,' he said, grinning broadly. 'What do you think of my daughter, eh? Quite a catch, eh – in more ways than one!' He laughed at his own words.

'I was trying to persuade her to show me over this place,' Matt returned easily. 'It's quite a place, sir.'

'Glad you like it. Designed it myself,' Stephen said proudly.

41

Matt grinned. 'You'll admit that you stole the idea from the Deep South, though, sir.'

'Of course I will!' Stephen clapped him on the shoulder. 'An architecture I admire very much. Gracious living and money to burn, eh? Don't you get that impression from the appearance of this house – just like the mansions in the Deep South? Well, I'm not ashamed of my money and I don't mind advertising that I'm a wealthy man. I don't mind telling you, my boy, that Promise will have a very healthy bank balance when she marries, too.'

'Father!' The exclamation was forced from Promise. She threw him an annoyed glance.

He threw his arm about her bare shoulders and drew her towards him, kissing her cheek affectionately. 'Your money won't scare Matt away if that's what worries you?'

She drew herself up haughtily. 'I can believe that.'

'Off you go! Show Matt the place – and don't forget to take him into the gardens. It's a lovely night and the moon is out!' He chuckled richly as Promise stalked from the room with Matt on her heels.

CHAPTER THREE

'What are you trying to do? Marry Promise to that Canadian?' Brent demanded as his father chuckled.

Stephen turned to him. 'Why not? He's a fine fellow and doesn't call any man his master. He won't even take orders from me and I pay his salary, damn him!' He smiled merrily at the thought.

'She doesn't like him.'

'Eh? What's that?'

'I said Promise doesn't like him,' Brent repeated.

'Nonsense! There's nothing about him to dislike.' He frowned briefly. 'He's just the man to handle Promise – he won't put up with her tantrums and she won't be able to twist him round her finger like she does with me. Yes, he's just the man for Promise and you'll find she agrees before the year's out.' He nodded affably to his son and went from the room.

Moodily, Brent tossed off his drink and slammed the empty glass on the bar. Impassively, a barman moved to refill it but he waved him away. 'Not now.' He walked to the door and stood surveying the crowded ballroom. Then he crossed the floor and pushed wide one of the open windows which led on to the terrace. Jonothan and Nancy were leaning against the stone balustrade and Jonothan was talking quietly but eagerly. He broke off as Brent stepped out of the window and his shoe grated on the stone floor.

'Sorry to break it up but Father wants you,' he said abruptly.

Jonothan hesitated briefly. Then he smiled warmly at the girl he loved. 'I won't be long. Wait here for me, Nancy.'

She nodded and watched as he went into the house. Then she turned to look at Brent, a slow smile curving her lips. She threw her head back and he looked hungrily at the slim, eager arch of her throat. With one step he was before her and his strong arms were about her slim, supple body. He pressed his lips hotly to her throat and then they strayed to her shoulder and down to the curve of her breast. She clung to him, her hands twined in the thick mass of his hair. The blood pounded in his veins and a tiny nerve throbbed in his cheek as he straightened up and looked down at her. A flood of passion swept through him. 'My God, you'll drive me mad!' he said huskily and caught her close once more. This time her lips were willing and eager for his kiss and he forgot everything but their sweetness, the warm desirability of her body so close to his. His hands were urgent and reckless, hurtful until she gave a little moan and pulled away from him.

'You're hurting me, Brent,' she said softly. 'You're so strong.'

His laugh was exultant on the night air. 'Strong! Of course I am. A damn sight stronger than Jonothan. He isn't a man and never will be. You need a man with hot red blood in his veins.'

She caught one of his hands and lifted it to her lips briefly. 'I know I do, Brent.'

He snatched his hand away. 'For heaven's sake! Keep those sentimental gestures for Jonothan – he appreciates them, I don't! Kiss me, you tempting little bitch!' He kissed her fiercely, heedless of the warm blood which flowed from his cut lip and tasted sweet to each of them. When he released her, his eyes were glowing. 'Has Jonothan ever kissed you like that? I'll say not. Milk and water in his veins if I'm any judge. What he knows about women wouldn't cover his thumbnail!'

She moved away from him abruptly. 'You don't love me, Brent,' she said slowly. 'You just want me – as if I were any woman.'

His eyes narrowed. 'You're not the kind of woman a man loves, Nancy. Only for a few hours, anyway – when you're warm and pliable in his arms. If you want sickly, sentimental emotion then stick to Jonothan. If you want passion and fire, then stick around and I'll supply both.'

Jonothan, pale and tense, stood motionless by the window. He felt sick with shock and bitter hatred of his brother. He could neither move nor speak – but as Brent pulled Nancy to him and bent his head to kiss her, he found his voice.

'Take your hands off her, Brent!' The command rang out crisply and with surprising authority. His voice sounded amazingly like his father's and Brent spun round swiftly, releasing Nancy. Then he laughed as he saw Jonothan.

'What's wrong? Can't a man kiss his future sister-in-law?' He slipped his arm about her as he spoke.

Jonothan clenched his fists and took a step forward. 'I told you to leave her alone, you filthy swine. There's only one reason why you'd want to kiss Nancy and no man, least of all my brother, is going to maul my fiancée without protest from me!'

Mocking him with his eyes, Brent assumed a sparring stance. 'What are you going to do? Black my eye?'

He was startled when Jonothan's fist shot out abruptly and caught him just below the eye. It was the first time he had ever known his younger brother to raise his hand to anyone. He was so stunned that he could only stare at Jonothan – but then, as the boy followed the first blow with another to his ribs, anger ripped through him and he let fly a right to Jonothan's chin. Nancy screamed as Jonothan went flying and fell heavily to the ground.

Brent stood over him, breathing hard, heedless of the curious crowd who came to the window. Stephen Power elbowed his way through and reached the terrace. He looked from Brent to the still body of his youngest son. Then, without a word, he lifted the boy in his arms and carried him back into the ballroom.

Brent turned his back on the staring faces and gripped his hands over the balustrade. Nancy began to shiver.

'Do you think he's very hurt?'

'Don't be a fool! I only stunned him. He'll be all right in a few moments.'

'Brent, how could you hit him? He's lame!' she cried.

'Shut up!' he growled fiercely. 'He struck the first blow, remember.'

'He had every right to do it, too,' she said with some heat.

He threw her a contemptuous glance. 'No need to be righteous with me, Nancy. You were as willing to be kissed as I was to kiss you. Do you want me to tell Jonothan that? If you still want to marry him, better to let him think that I was molesting you.'

She was silent for a long moment. Then quietly, so quietly that he barely caught the words, she said: 'Oh, Brent, don't you know that I love you? How can I marry Jonothan?'

He stared at her. Then he shrugged. 'That's your affair.' He went to walk away but his father called his name harshly and he turned.

Stephen Power stepped on to the terrace. His face was set and angry. Stripping off his coat and tie, he said icily: 'If you must fight, get your coat off.'

Brent was startled. Despite his advantage of height, he knew he was no match for his father who was an exceedingly powerful man. 'Let's be sensible, Father,' he began.

Stephen interrupted him. 'Get your coat off.' He jerked his head at Nancy. 'Shouldn't you be with Jonothan?' he asked coldly. 'You don't want to watch this.'

Nancy hastily entered the house. Father and son stared at each other. Stephen turned, closed the window firmly and waited until Mathieson drew the heavy curtains. It was an ominous moment. The long terrace, bathed in moonlight, held only two figures – father and son. There was no doubt in Brent's mind that his father meant to teach him a lesson.

'We can't fight, Father,' he said un-certainly. 'We're not evenly matched. You're not a young man...'

He broke off as he received a heavy blow to the side of his head which made him stagger. 'Were you and Jonothan evenly-matched?' Stephen cried furiously. 'Get your fists up!'

It was a long and bitter struggle between the two men for supremacy. Angered by that unexpected blow, Brent was determined to make no allowances for his father – and he quickly found that he needed all his wits and all his skill to defend himself. Stephen

Power had learned how to fight in a hard school and there was little skill but much impact behind his blows. He had always been proud of his sons for knowing how to look after themselves in a fight but he was disgusted that Brent should lay hands on Jonothan no matter what the provocation and he was firmly decided that in future when he told his sons there was to be no fighting his word would be heeded. As he frequently boasted, he had the courage of a lion – and it seemed to Brent in those long, painful minutes that he had the hide of rhinoceros. He did not pull his punches but apart from one or two painful grunts his father scarcely heeded the blows which Brent landed. Respecting his good looks, Stephen aimed most of his blows at Brent's body but occasionally he landed a heavy one to his face or the side of his head.

Brent found that his added height was little advantage to him. Several of his hits went wide for his father was amazingly agile, weaving in and out of his guard, avoiding his blows with surprising ease. He completely forgot that it was his father who fought him and he used all his skill and all his strength to shake off the man who opposed him.

He doubled with pain as Stephen's knuckles caught him full in the pit of his stomach. The next moment, his head cracked back as his father hit him on the point of the chin. Slowly, he slumped to the ground and lay still.

Stephen waited a moment – then he stepped back and surveyed his son ruefully. He sucked his grazed knuckles and shook his head to clear it. Well, that should teach the boy a lesson!

Taking his shirt, coat and tie from the balustrade, he hastily slipped into them and then went into the house, buttoning his shirt. Immediately he was surrounded by people but he merely shook his head to all questions and pushed his way through them. He caught Mathieson's eye and nodded to him.

He strode across the room to Jonothan who still looked slightly dazed but was now on his feet and looking better. 'How do you feel?' he asked kindly and in his eyes was a new-found admiration for the boy who had dared to tackle his older, taller and stronger brother in a good cause.

'I'm all right, Father,' Jonothan returned impatiently. 'Where's Brent? Someone said you were fighting on the terrace.'

'That's right. He's out cold at the moment.' He nodded briefly and walked over to the orchestra who were talking excitedly. 'Let's have some music,' he ordered. 'That's what you're paid for!'

Within seconds, music filled the room and Stephen circulated among his guests, assuring them that everything was in hand and apologising for the brief disturbance. It did not worry him that his left eye was rapidly changing colour and that a fine trickle of blood ran from one of his nostrils...

Promise walked with Matt in the gardens, bored but obedient to her father's last words although she had entertained every intention of coldly refusing Matt's suggestion. They walked in silence for she had exhausted her eulogies on the home she had known all her life and he had long ago run out of complimentary remarks.

A high hedge on either side hid the house from view as they turned into a small lane between two expanses of cultivated flower-beds.

'This is deserted enough,' he commented. 'A lover's lane of our own? We ought to put it to good use.' Before she realised his intention, he had his arms about her and his hand beneath her chin, forcing her face up with his strong, sensitive fingers. She struggled vainly, angry and startled.

He smiled mockingly. 'Isn't this why you brought me out here? You're quick enough to take the hint from your old man.'

'How dare you!' she gasped, words almost failing her in her temper. 'If you don't let me go this minute, I'll … I'll…'

He laughed. 'What *will* you do? Slap my face? But that's just following tradition, isn't it? I don't mind. Go ahead and slap. It won't be the first time a lovely girl has walloped me for trying to kiss her!'

'If my father knew, he'd horsewhip you!' she cried.

'Really? Now that would be a new experience,' he said musingly.

'You're despicable,' she cried, renewing her struggles to free herself.

'Maybe – but I'm not a fool, Promise Power. You can put on a pretty show of fear but you don't deceive me. You can hardly wait to be kissed.'

'Oh!' Adroitly releasing one hand, she dealt him a resounding blow across the cheek – then she coloured furiously as she realised that she had fulfilled his expectations and that he was laughing at her. 'If I never see you again it will be too soon!' she stormed.

'You've plenty of spirit,' he commented smoothly. 'I like that in a woman. You know, I don't know whether to kiss you now or postpone the pleasurable moment and leave you in suspense.'

'You'll never get another chance!' she cried.

He regarded her thoughtfully. 'I doubt that – but perhaps I'd better not take the risk.' Suddenly, he caught her even closer and pressed his mouth hard upon hers. Tense, furious, her whole body tautened with anger and she moved her mouth enough to sink her teeth deeply into his lower lip.

He released her abruptly and whipped out a white handkerchief which he pressed to his bleeding mouth. 'The action of a lady,' he said coldly.

'Another new experience?' she tautened, delighted with her prompt action. 'If I were a lady, you wouldn't have thought of trying to kiss me,' she went on angrily, and then she glared at him as she realised the admission of her words.

'Exactly,' he murmured. 'You're not a lady – and no amount of money or fine airs will make you one. I detest a woman who leads a man on and then pretends that she doesn't want to be kissed when he decides to oblige her.'

'That isn't true!' she snapped.

He looked at her for a long moment until she lowered her lashes quickly. She disliked the shrewd penetration of his dark eyes. 'So you lie to yourself, do you.' It was not a question.

The blunt statement annoyed her intensely. 'I think we'd better go in,' she said icily and walked off, leaving him. He hesitated then he strode after her, catching her arm.

'Aren't you going to apologise?' he demanded, bringing her to a standstill.

She looked up at him innocently. 'For biting you? But, Mr Nellin – you shouldn't have kissed me.'

'How am I going to explain this?' He touched his bleeding underlip angrily.

'Tell the truth, of course. My father will be most amused,' she threw at him.

He held and locked her gaze and there was something infinitely disturbing in his eyes. She felt a tiny shiver travel down her spine. 'I'll break your spirit,' he said quietly. 'If it's the last thing I ever do, I'll break your spirit,

Promise Power.' He grabbed her arm again, angrily this time. 'Come on! You're neglecting your friends!' The words were a sneer, and oddly enough Promise was hurt by his tone.

They went back to the house without a word being exchanged between them and the first thing Promise saw as they mounted the terrace steps was her brother Brent being doused with a bucket of water by an impassive Mathieson. She looked at Matt – and then hurried on, annoyed that there had been trouble while she was absent and partly disappointed that she should have missed it!

Shocked, she caught sight of her father's face as he turned towards them as they entered the ballroom. She flew to his side.

'Whatever's happened?'

He smiled and patted her hand which she had placed on his arm. 'Nothing to worry about, Promise. Brent got out of hand and I put him in his place.'

Her eyes widened. 'You and Brent were fighting?'

He laughed. 'It isn't the first time, is it?'

'No-o...' she admitted. 'But why?' she demanded immediately.

'We had a slight disagreement.' That was

all he would say and he turned to Matt Nellin. 'Well, my boy, did Promise show you everything.' He leaned forward and looked intently at Matt. Then he grinned broadly. 'I guess you found that my little rose has a few thorns, Matt.'

Dark colour stained the man's face. He met Stephen's eyes levelly. 'More than a few, sir.'

He turned to look closely at Promise. 'A fine way to treat a guest, my dear.'

She tossed her head. 'You're too observant, Father.'

He chuckled. 'I keep my eyes open, don't I? Have to with a brood like mine. Always in trouble.' He met Matt's eyes and smiled. 'Not too tight a rein but a firm hand, my boy. Let them know who's master. They all have minds of their own and plenty of spirit but I handle them well enough.'

'Perhaps you'll give me a few lessons, sir,' Matt said drily. 'I'm afraid I found your prize filly much too restless to hold.'

Stephen roared with laughter. 'Perhaps you startled her, my boy. She's very highly-strung and you have to coax her to take fences.'

Promise moved impatiently. Matt glanced at her. Her eyes blazed and she tilted her chin indignantly. He smiled briefly but without warmth.

Stephen patted his shoulder. 'You shouldn't rush her, you know, Matt. She's a shy little thing.' Promise threw him an angry look which he ignored. 'Don't be deceived by her looks and her manners.'

'I'm not, sir,' Matt said firmly and gave Promise a look which she could only construe in one way.

Later that evening, in the privacy of her bedroom, she threw herself face down on her bed and closed her eyes to the recurring image of Matt Nellin's face.

'I hate him!' she said aloud, vehemently. 'I hate him!'

For all her faults, she was honest with herself and breaking through the angry hatred came the realisation that she was only furious because he had so quickly pierced the veneer of her shy demurity in a way that no man had ever done before. Without hesitation he had summed her up and known that at heart she was a woman who enjoyed the company of men, appreciated to the full her power over them and considered herself well able to keep them exactly where she wanted them! He had perceived the wanton streak in her character and known that she would not be averse to his love-making despite the fact that she scarcely knew him. His mistake had been in acting too quickly, in betraying his instinctive knowledge of her innermost self and in taunting her beyond the limits of her self-control.

CHAPTER FOUR

Brent moodily divested himself of his evening clothes. The muscles rippled in his tall, magnificent and sun-bronzed body. He was more than a little drunk and his present black mood was born of humiliation that his own father, a man thirty years older than himself and certainly not in excellent condition, had managed to knock him out in a fight. He had not returned to the ballroom but spent the rest of the evening in the library with a bottle of whiskey brought to him by an openly-disapproving Mathieson.

An abrupt knock on his door brought him from his reverie. 'Come in!' he shouted and the door opened to reveal Jonothan standing on the threshold of the room, hesitant but determined. 'Well, what the hell do you want?' Brent demanded coldly.

'I want to talk to you,' Jonothan returned.

'Well, come in, man – and shut the door! Do you want one of the maids to pass by and see me standing here naked.' He snatched up a robe and pulled it on as

Jonothan entered the room and closed the door behind him, standing with his back to the panels.

'You're drunk,' Jonothan said quietly.

'Not for the first time. What do you expect? Do you think a man can take a beating from his own father in a fair fight and not get drunk?' He sat down heavily in a chair, helped himself to a cigarette and stared at his young brother. 'Well, get on with it. I'm listening.'

'Do you feel all right?' Jonothan asked anxiously.

Brent grinned. 'Sure. It's not the first time I've been out for the count – although it doesn't happen often.'

'Was it a fair fight?' Jonothan wanted to know.

'Of course.'

'You didn't *let* Father knock you out?'

Brent laughed harshly. 'Are you kidding? It took me all my time to stand up to him. You've never had a battle royal with him, have you? He's no boxer but he can certainly pack a punch!'

'I'm afraid it was all my fault,' Jonothan said quietly. 'I'm sorry, Brent. I shouldn't have hit you.'

'Idiot! You couldn't hurt a fly. Are *you* all

right?' He looked a little sheepish as he added ungraciously: 'I didn't mean to hit you so hard, Jon.'

'I've been talking to Nancy,' he said dully, ignoring the half-apology.

Brent's eyes narrowed. 'So?'

'I didn't know,' he said and there was a gleam of sadness in his eyes.

'Didn't know what?'

'That you and Nancy were in love,' he went on in that same expressionless tone.

Brent stared at him. 'She told you that!'

He nodded. 'She broke our engagement. Told me that you were the one she really cared for – and that you hadn't been molesting her on the terrace. I decided I ought to apologise to you, Brent.'

Brent rose and began to pace the room. With a swift movement he stubbed his cigarette. 'The artful little devil!' he murmured under his breath with a tinge of admiration in his tone. Aloud, he said: 'What else did Nancy tell you?'

'That you wanted to marry her – that you've always wanted to marry her but wouldn't hurt me by letting me know. You should have told me, Brent. I wouldn't have stood in your way. Nancy's happiness is all that matters to me – and I'd rather know she was married to my own brother than anyone else.'

Brent pulled thoughtfully at his lip. 'That's very generous of you, Jon,' he said awkwardly, wondering what else he was supposed to say and completely baffled by the turn of events. 'But I've no intention of marrying Nancy.'

Jonothan's fists clenched. 'But you must. Don't think of me, Brent.'

'I'm thinking of myself, thanks,' Brent said dryly.

His meaning suddenly sank into Jonothan's brain and he took a step forward. 'You've got to marry Nancy,' he said harshly. 'She's going to have a baby!'

Brent stood stockstill and his fuddled brain cleared with abrupt precipitance. 'What did you say?'

'She told me tonight. Nancy's going to have a child – your child.'

Brent's face was white and his eyes were very dark. 'It isn't mine,' he said curtly.

'It must be. She said it is. It certainly isn't mine,' Jonothan returned proudly.

'Damn the bitch! She can't do this to me!' Brent exclaimed furiously.

Jonothan paled visibly. 'Then you don't love her?'

'Be your age! She's told you a pack of lies.'

'I believe her,' he affirmed stoutly. He eyed his brother with disgust and contempt. 'I knew you were pretty rotten, Brent – but I thought you'd draw the line somewhere!'

'For God's sake! Must you talk to me as though we were schoolboys together, you little prig! I can believe that you're too damned innocent to father the brat but why should you believe Nancy's story that I'm the father?'

'It's possible, isn't it?'

'Assuming the child is mine, what makes you think I'll marry her?' Brent shouted angrily. 'A substantial cheque will satisfy the girl!'

Stephen stood in the doorway and his gaze was unpleasant as it rested on his son who swung round at the opening of the door and glowered at him.

'People are trying to sleep,' Stephen said quietly. 'Go to your room, Jonothan.'

'But, Father…'

'Go to your room,' came the adamant reply and reluctantly Jonothan walked out, his father holding the door open for him.

'I suppose you heard,' Brent said.

'What do you expect when you raise the roof with your voice? I could hear you clearly in my room. Now what's it all about? Is it true that Nancy Armstrong is expecting your child?'

'How should I know?' Brent demanded sullenly.

'Is it possible?'

'Me and a dozen others,' he retorted, 'could answer yes to that!'

'Nonsense! The girl was decent enough till you cast your eyes in her direction. I've been suspicious for some months. Haven't you any affection for your brother at all that you had to interfere in his affairs? Why did you have to pick on the girl he loves?'

'Does it occur to you that Nancy was a willing party?'

'You can be very persuasive, my son. But you should have more sense. You'll marry Nancy Armstrong within the month – or you can pack your things and get out!'

'You don't mean that,' Brent jeered.

Stephen's lips tightened. 'I mean every word of it, Brent!' He strode from the room and closed the door firmly behind him.

Back in his own bedroom, he loosened the cord of his robe and slipped between the sheets. Lying in the darkness, his eyes wide open, he pondered the problem of his children. He wondered if he was to blame for their recklessness, their lack of thought for the feelings of others, their immoral approach to life.

Adam. His firstborn son. Tall, handsome with the Power looks, red hair and grey eyes and clean cut features, powerful and intelligent – and now nearing thirty. The fruit of his first year of marriage to Susannah. A man to admire and to take a pride in – but a man without much sense of responsibility. It was time he married and settled down. As the eldest he should have strived to set his brothers a good example: instead he was usually the ringleader in all their pranks. But they were all growing too old for foolishness. Adam was an industrious son when he chose and he was the right-hand man in the business – but he seldom chose to put in a full day's work five days a week.

Russell. The second son and equally as handsome and powerfully built as Adam. Two years younger but always matching in height and strength from early childhood. As reckless as the others but with a little more consideration and an innate sense of responsibility which needed only slight encouragement to be active. An intelligent man with a good head for mathematics and he was almost as useful as Adam to the business. But he had no heart in the company and his fist love was his black stallion and the stables.

Brent. The third son. He and Russell could almost be twins and there was scarcely a year between their ages. He had always been the wildest, the most daring, the most violent, even if Adam and Russ had never been far behind. He drank too much and he was proud of his conquests where women were concerned. A rebellious man with a chip on his shoulder. It might be the best thing for him to be sent away to make something of his life. Certainly marrying him off to Nancy Armstrong would be a mistake despite the girl's evident infatuation for him.

Promise. His only and beloved daughter. She intrigued him greatly for he did not understand the way her mind worked. She was beautiful with great charm and personality, warm-hearted and appealing, persuasive and intelligent. She frequently baffled him for he was convinced that few people knew the real person and he wondered why she felt that she had to adopt a pretence. She was much liked and much admired – but she was as rebellious in her own way as Brent and he knew that it would

67

be a relief when she was married to a man who loved, understood and controlled her despite the loss it would be to himself.

Jonothan. His youngest child. He had long since recovered from the shock of his lameness and the grief that his birth had caused Susannah's death. He loved the boy but he could never reach him. He was too introverted for his age, too wrapped up in his books and studies and music, too timid for the violence of the world about him. He thought of the way Jonothan had squared up to Brent that evening and a smile touched his lips. The boy had courage, anyway – but none of the Powers were lacking in that quality.

Five children – a quiverful, as he had been wont to remark when they were small. Now he freely admitted that they were a handful and he decided that he must be getting old if he could no longer keep a firm hand on the reins. He had warned Brent that there was to be no fighting but the boy had defied him. It had been a shock to discover that Jonothan was the victim of his attack but he had soon learned that Nancy Armstrong was at the root of their disagreement.

He had nothing against Nancy. He quite liked the girl although he did not approve of her as a wife for Jonothan, considering them both too young to know their own minds. He was not concerned with their ages. He had been younger than Jonothan when he married Susannah. It was experience of the world that mattered and Jonothan was very lacking in that. Nancy knew little of the world apart from her immediate surroundings and the nearby small towns.

Despite the fact that Nancy had told Jonothan she was expecting a child by Brent, he did not believe it was the truth. He had suspected for several months that Brent was amusing himself with the girl behind Jonothan's back but he felt convinced that Brent was not that much of a fool. It was conceivably a ruse on Nancy's part to force Brent into marrying her – and Stephen Power was not going to allow that.

He regretted now that he had delivered the ultimatum to Brent before he knew the truth of Nancy's claim. But he would soon find out for himself whether or not she was speaking the truth...

She faced him squarely the following morning. It was another warm day and the windows of the library were opened wide and fastened. He looked through the window, choosing his words carefully. She waited. She had been surprised by the summons but it did not occur to her to ignore them.

She waited. At last he turned to her.

'Why do you want to marry Brent, Nancy?'

Startled, the colour flooded her face. 'Because I love him,' she said stoutly.

'Do you? How old are you, Nancy?'

'Nineteen.'

'So young? And so sure of your feelings? I wonder why Brent appeals to you? Is it his brute force? His magnetism? His lack of respect for convention? His madcap ways?'

'I don't know,' she said and her tone was almost sullen.

'I was willing for you to marry Jonothan because you're well suited to each other. But Brent will never make you a good husband. Do you realise that, Nancy? He drinks too much. He'll chase other women before you've been married a month. He has no sense of responsibility. One of these days, with all his fighting, he'll go too far and find himself in court for manslaughter. Is that the kind of husband you want? A man like Brent who doesn't even love you?'

'He does!' she exclaimed furiously.

'I'm not Jonothan, you know. You can't tell

me a pack of lies and get away with it.' He paused and then fired an abrupt question at her: 'When do you expect this baby?'

Taken aback, she said hastily: 'November.'

He looked her up and down and again her face was bright with embarrassment. 'Really? You don't look pregnant to me – and I do have some experience of these matters, if you'll believe me? Why are you trying to trap Brent into marriage? Don't you know that he'll never marry you?'

She dissolved into tears, knuckling her eyes like a small child. He watched her and his eyes softened a little.

'You've been a silly girl, Nancy,' he said quietly. 'You're not going to have a baby, are you?'

She shook her head. 'No.'

'More by luck than judgment, I'll wager,' he said drily. 'However, that isn't my business. If you've any sense you'll tell Jonothan the truth. I'm not saying anything about your decision to break your engagement to him. I don't think you'd be happy with any of my sons, my dear. But, you know, you were flying a little too high when you set your cap at Brent.'

'You won't tell my father,' she pleaded anxiously, her tears abating swiftly.

He shrugged. 'Why should I? Your morals are no concern of mine. You used to be a nice little thing. It's a pity you happened to attract Brent, even if briefly; you're not his type at all, you know.'

'I do love him!' she exclaimed.

'At the moment. But in six months' time you'll wonder why you were ever such a fool as to think so, my dear. One can say many things of Brent – but not that he's lovable! No woman has ever loved Brent – and that's partly his trouble, don't you agree? Off you go, my dear. We've settled the whole matter satisfactorily.' He picked up a newspaper and relaxed comfortably in his chair. She did not move and he looked up again. 'Well?'

'What about me?' she asked indignantly.

'That's your problem,' he told her firmly. 'If you want to go on seeing Brent, it doesn't concern me – but I don't think you'll find he's interested in you any longer. No one in my family cares for liars!' He nodded to her and returned to his newspaper.

Bereft of words, she left the room – and met Brent himself as he crossed the hall, dressed in riding kit and slapping his thigh with his crop. He looked at her then walked by her without a word.

'Brent!' She said his name hungrily.

He turned. 'Yes.' He was curt and cold.

'You can't treat me like this!' she cried. 'It isn't fair!'

'My poor child, what can you do about it?' he asked calmly. 'If you could prove it's my child, I might be interested – but I haven't that much faith in your morals!'

She swayed beneath the blow of his words. 'Oh, Brent – how can you say that! There's never been any man but you – you know that! Anyway,' she added sulkily, 'I was wrong. There isn't any baby.'

His expression changed miraculously. His eyes brightened and a swift smile touched his lips. 'Well, that's a relief. What on earth made you say so if you weren't sure? Do you realise that I was nearly thrown out on my ear because of you?'

'I suppose you didn't even care if it was true,' she accused.

'Should I? It probably isn't the first I've fathered – although I admit it's the first time I've been named.' He grinned mischievously.

With one swift movement she seized his riding crop from his hand and laid it about his head and shoulders. His hands went up quickly to protect his head and he shouted

73

with pain as she lashed him angrily. The library door was opened abruptly and Stephen strode forward, taking in the situation at a glance. He wrenched the crop from Nancy's hand, his eyes grim. 'That's quite enough!' he snapped icily.

Nancy looked at Brent, her eyes full of loathing, then she ran across the hall and through the open door of the house.

Brent raised his head. Lifting his fingers to his cheek, he looked at the blood which stained them when he removed them. 'Damned spitfire!' he said without malice. Then he grinned. 'I didn't know she could do such a thing,' he said and his voice held a note of admiration.

'Why the hell did I ever have sons?' Stephen asked bitterly. He threw the crop to the floor at Brent's feet and walked away.

Brent looked after him, wrinkling his brow. Then he stooped to pick up the crop and walked upstairs to his room, whistling beneath his breath.

CHAPTER FIVE

Russ sauntered leisurely across the cobbles and entered the stables, whistling the tune of a ribald song. Adam finished buckling the girth of his saddle before he turned his head to nod to his younger brother. Russ walked up to his own black stallion.

'Where's Brent?' Adam asked impatiently.

'He went back to the house for something.' He stroked the long, sleek nose of his horse, fed him a lump of sugar which he took from his pocket and then turned to heave down the heavy saddle. 'You're out early. I thought you'd be sleeping off the effects of last night. What time did you get back?'

Adam's dark, heavy eyebrows lowered. He was peculiarly sensitive about his association with Julie Wentworth. He had few illusions about her character but he had convinced Brent of his folly in blackening her name and he was fully prepared to do the same for Russ if he said one word out of place.

'That's my business,' he returned curtly.

Russ grinned. He studied the faint shadows under Adam's eyes with cool insolence. 'Was it worth the drive?' He began to fasten the leather straps of the saddle. 'She's quite a hot number, isn't she?'

'Is she?' Adam growled resentfully.

'Didn't you find that out for yourself. Perhaps she's more selective than I thought – or else she prefers my company to yours!'

Adam took a step towards him. 'What do you mean by that?'

Russ opened his eyes wide in mock innocence. 'Didn't she tell you of our drive to the coast last week? Why, that's too bad of Julie! I felt sure she wouldn't forget it in a hurry!' The angry look in Adam's eyes boded ill for him but he was undisturbed, anticipating with a thrill of pleasure a brief but telling fracas with his brother to blow away the morning cobwebs.

'I ought to knock your head off,' Adam said harshly.

'Go ahead,' Russ grinned.

Adam clenched his fist – then changed his mind and turned his back on Russ. He led the stallion out of his stall and into the open and then swung up into the saddle. Russ looked after him, puzzled. He knew how sensitive Adam was where Julie Wentworth was concerned but for some reason or another he had not risen to the bait for once. He mentally shrugged and busied himself with getting his horse ready for the morning gallop.

They began nearly every day with a ride, vying with each other for supremacy in the saddle and showing off the prowess of their individual horses.

Russ was surprised when he led his horse out of the stable to find that his brother had already galloped away and was some distance off. As Brent walked towards him, he leaped into the saddle and waved a hand towards his brother.

'Are you waiting for me?' Brent asked as he drew level with him.

Russ nodded. 'Adam was in the devil of a hurry. He's in a foul mood this morning. Couldn't even persuade him to mix it a bit,' he said ruefully, remembering the disappointment he had known as Adam turned away, evidently in no mood to fight. Suddenly he leaned down and looked intently at his brother's face. A thin weal showing a tiny ooze of blood marked his left cheek. 'Who the devil did that?' he demanded angrily.

Brent touched his cheek which was more

than a little painful but no worse than other marks he had received in the past – but it was the first one he had received from a woman's hand. 'That,' he said carelessly. 'Oh, that was Nancy.'

Russ stared in surprise. 'Nancy?'

'Mm. We had a slight disagreement.' He grinned at the memory. 'She seized my crop and dealt me a couple of stingers. I guess I annoyed her.'

'I should think you did,' Russ said vehemently, anger flaring. 'What on earth happened between you?'

'Nothing important. I happened to say something she didn't like.' He dismissed the subject and went into the stable leaving Russ to fume at the thought of a chit like Nancy Armstrong daring to strike his brother. In an ugly mood when Brent came out of the stables, he scarcely waited for his brother to mount before he touched his stallion's rump with his crop and urged him into a gallop. Brent leaped into the saddle and went after him at breakneck speed...

There was no sign of Adam and they soon decided to make their own way without bothering about him. 'Let him stew in his own juice for a while,' Brent shouted above the high wind which marred an otherwise glorious summer day. 'I guess Julie didn't live up to expectations, after all.'

Russ grinned but made no answer. He knew a wild exhilaration as he rode against the wind which lifted his auburn hair and whipped fresh colour into his handsome face. His horse was his main love in life and he was never happier than when he was in the saddle with the ground slipping away swiftly beneath his stallion's nimble hooves and excitement filling his veins.

Brent had a difficult time to keep up with him and eventually he slackened the pace, having more respect for his horse who could not compete with Swift.

Losing sight of Russ, he turned his mount's head and cantered back towards the village at an easy pace. It was not un-usual for the brothers to split up during the morning ride and neither interfered at any time with any decision made by one of the others. He had a strong suspicion that Russ was heading for a small pub a few miles outside the village with the hope of meeting the young and impressionable daughter of the publican. Brent had looked the girl over for himself but decided that she was not his type so he was content to leave the field open to Russ.

His thoughts turned idly to Nancy Armstrong as his horse slithered in a pothole and jerked him in his seat, causing his cheek to throb slightly. He had been shocked but amused by her attack and he had known a faint admiration for the sudden show of spirit. She had not interested him very much at first and he had dismissed her as being just the type that Jonothan would prefer. Gradually, as the weeks passed and he met her more frequently at the house or in the grounds, he began to feel a spark of interest as she turned her unusual amber eyes upon him – eyes that glowed strangely whenever he appeared on the scene.

He had seized an opportunity to kiss her one evening when Jonothan went into the house to fetch a book he wanted her to see, fully expecting a rebuff. To his surprise, she had returned his kiss ardently and hungrily and he had felt passion rising swiftly. Twining his fingers painfully in her hair, he bent her head back and buried his lips in her throat. Then thrusting down the low-necked blouse she wore he had fiercely kissed the soft curve of her breast. Giving a little moan she had pulled him close to her and he had known instinctively that he could have whatever he wanted from her – at another more opportune moment. Knowing the thrill of yet another conquest and the promise of future pleasures, he had released her abruptly and left her as Jonothan came limping from the house with a warm smile for Nancy and the book in his hand, quite unsuspecting.

Their meetings had been clandestine and all the more enjoyable because of it – and because he had little love for anyone and scant respect for his young brother, he exulted in the knowledge that Nancy was secretly his mistress while apparently planning to marry his brother. Usually, he tired of women within a matter of weeks – but there was something intoxicating about Nancy which appealed to him even more than the whiskey which satisfied some strange part of his make-up and he had continued the deceit for the last few months without a thought for the eventual outcome.

He had been furious on the previous night when Jonothan came to his room and told him what had taken place between Nancy and himself. Marriage had been the last thought he entertained and he was determined that no woman should trap him into that snare, least of all a woman like Nancy. He had been fully prepared to pack his things and leave his home at his father's order but it had been a relief to learn that the girl was lying.

He cantered down the quiet lane, a thoughtful smile wreathing his lips. It was unlikely that Nancy would ever speak to him again but there were plenty of other women and she was not important to him. His pride smarted a little that she had turned on him but he was honest enough to admit that he had given her ample provocation.

He reined his horse abruptly as Nancy stepped from behind the hedge and stood squarely in the lane. He looked down at her. 'Well?'

'I want to talk to you, Brent Power,' she said and she almost spat his name from her lips.

He grinned. 'Talk away.'

'Get down.'

He raised an eyebrow. 'I'm quite comfortable here, thanks. Whatever you have to say to me can't take very long.'

She thrust her hand into the deep pocket of her riding breeches and pulled out a small automatic revolver which she pointed at him squarely. 'Get down.'

His face turned an ugly colour. 'What the

devil...! Put that thing away, Nancy. Are you mad?'

'I could shoot you in the saddle but I'd hate to miss and kill your horse,' she said coldly.

He leaped from the saddle and before she could move or protest whipped the gun from her hand. She struggled to retrieve it, pummelling his powerful chest. With one hand he held her away from him while he examined the gun and with some relief found that she had not released the safety catch.

'You don't know much about guns, do you?' he asked mockingly.

Tears welled to her eyes and streamed down her cheeks soundlessly. 'Do you think I wanted to kill you?' she asked quietly. 'I only wanted to frighten you!'

He laughed. 'Powers don't scare easily, my dear girl.' His grip on her arm tightened. 'I ought to beat the daylights out of you,' he said harshly.

She caught her breath and put her hand up to his cheek. 'Oh, Brent!' she cried. 'Did I do that?'

'It was only a glancing blow – or I'd have been scarred for life,' he said grimly. 'Maybe that's what you wanted.' He shook her suddenly, fiercely. 'You must be mad! First attacking me with my crop – and now threatening to shoot me. What's the matter with you?'

Her eyes were desperate in their appeal. 'I love you, Brent. I love you so much. I can't bear it if you leave me.'

His laugh was an ugly, mocking sound. 'Leave you? I don't belong to you, Nancy. Get that into your head, will you? You're nothing to me – nothing!'

She bowed her head while the tears still flowed. 'How can you be so cruel?'

'How can you be so stupid?' he retorted. 'I've told you – you're not the first girl in my life and you're not likely to be the last. It doesn't mean a thing. Just pleasant company for a few hours – a brief interlude. Like every woman, you think I should be tied to you for life because you've been my mistress.'

She pulled her arm away and began to run, blindly, almost stumbling. Brent looked after her and then shrugged. He turned to his horse, caught the reins and was about to mount when the sound of a car caught his attention. He turned his head as the car turned into the lane, moving at speed towards Nancy who ran on, seeming not to notice the car. He shouted her name – and then, horrified, leaped into the saddle and galloped after her. The driver threw on the brakes and tore at the steering wheel as Nancy made no effort to avoid the oncoming car.

A few moments of confusion. Then the car lurched drunkenly in the ditch and Nancy lay stunned. The side of the car had caught and thrown her. Brent was off the horse and stooping over her in a moment.

Promise scrambled from the car, pale and horrified – and then supremely angry as she realised that Nancy was scarcely hurt.

'The stupid little fool!' she blurted. 'Is she all right?'

'No bones broken, anyway,' Brent said curtly, running his hands expertly over the slight body.

'Why on earth did she run towards me like that? Couldn't she see me?' Promise demanded. 'She might have been killed!'

'Are you all right?' Brent asked, turning to his sister.

She nodded and laughed shakily. 'It was a nasty moment, though. This lane is too narrow for tricky manoeuvres.'

'What possessed you to drive down this lane, anyway?' Brent asked angrily as he lifted Nancy in his arms. He was almost trembling from the shock and confusion of the incident.

'You know it's a short cut to the arterial road,' she protested. 'I'm going up to Town.' She looked ruefully at the white sports car. 'At least, that was my intention. What am I supposed to do about my car?'

Brent's glance was merely cursory. 'You won't shift it from there without garage help.'

'What are you going to do about Nancy?'

'Ride to the village and knock up Wilson. What else? I don't think she's hurt, really. Just stunned. But I'm not taking any chances.'

Promise glanced at her brother curiously. 'Were you quarrelling?'

'Mind your own business,' he said rudely. 'I'm going to put her on the back seat of your car. You'd better stay with her while I fetch Wilson.'

'I've an appointment in Town,' Promise objected.

'Too bad. You'll have to break it, won't you,' he said shortly.

She opened the door to the back seat. 'I might have known something would prevent me from carrying out my plans. Go on,

Brent. I'll stay with her. You'd better tell Bill Hurry to bring his breakdown van – perhaps he'll give you a lift back with Wilson.'

It seemed an eternity before Nancy stirred and Promise was feeling anxious. But at last the girl opened her eyes and raised a hand to the side of her head. 'What happened?' she asked shakily.

'You're lucky that you're alive to ask,' Promise told her grimly. 'I nearly ran you over, you idiot. Surely you could see the car?'

'I didn't care,' she said dully. 'I wanted to die.'

Promise gasped. 'Why? Why should you think like that, Nancy?' She bent over the girl and smoothed the dark hair from her brow. 'What's wrong, dear?' she asked gently.

She moved her head restlessly. 'Nothing. Please don't question me. It doesn't matter now, anyway.'

'Do you feel all right?' Promise asked anxiously.

Nancy looked at her and seemed to recognise her fully for the first time. A painful, bitter smile twisted her lips. 'It would be your car, of course. It's impossible to move five yards without running into a

Power, isn't it?'

Promise frowned. 'You're damn lucky it *was* my car! Not many people could have handled a car with enough skill to avoid killing you, my girl.'

'The colossal conceit of the Powers,' Nancy murmured bitterly. 'It never fails, does it.'

Promise flushed angrily. 'Perhaps you'd better not talk any more. Brent will be back with Dr Wilson in a few minutes. I don't want you passing out on me again.'

'Brent? Brent's gone for the doctor?' she asked swiftly, incredulously.

'Yes. Now lie quietly and don't talk,' Promise urged.

'Was he worried?' she asked softly. 'Just tell me that, Promise – and I'll be quiet.'

'Of course he was worried. You ran away from him and tried to get yourself killed by my car. Why, did you expect him to be jumping for joy?' Promise asked with cold irony.

Nancy made no reply but closed her eyes and relaxed on the leather seat. She ached all over and her head was throbbing. A deep-rooted misery pumped far-reaching pain from her heart and her brain repeated Brent's name silently again and again.

Promise was glad to see the breakdown van turn into the lane and still more pleased when it pulled up close behind the car and Brent and Dr Wilson stepped down to the ground. Bill Hurry thrust his head out of the window and grinned cheerfully at Promise.

'I should have known you'd be in trouble again, Miss,' he said lightly.

'Not my fault this time, Bill,' she returned with a smile.

It did not take long for Dr Wilson to make a quick, expert examination of Nancy and to receive satisfactory answers to his rapid questions. Brent waited, smoking a cigarette with impatient, restless movements, while Promise stood talking to Bill Hurry who evinced a curious interest in the accident to her car.

Wilson turned to Brent. 'There's nothing wrong with her. She's a little shocked, still – and she'll have a few bruises. She needs to spend the rest of the day in bed, that's all. I'm not needed here. You'll see that she gets home all right, Brent? I was on my way to a woman in labour and I can do more for her than for Nancy.'

'Bill will take you back to the village,' Brent said. 'I'll pay him for the extra time.

Promise isn't in any hurry for her car.'

Promise threw him an exasperated glance but made no protest. 'Shall I take the young lady home, too,' Bill suggested.

Brent considered for a moment. Then he shook his head. 'No, she can ride in front of me. It won't hurt her and I have a few things to say to her. But you can give Promise a lift home after you've dropped the doctor, if you will?'

He nodded. 'Sure. My time's at your disposal.'

'It should be. I'm paying for it,' Brent said curtly and turned to Nancy. 'Feel well enough to go home?' He did not meet her eyes.

She nodded miserably. 'I'm all right.'

'That isn't your fault,' he said curtly. He took her arm and led her forcibly to the patient horse who was idly grazing at the grassy bank. Brent mounted and gave a hand to Nancy, pulling her up to sit before him. The saddle was just wide enough for them both, Nancy crushed against his hard chest. He took the reins and they trotted gently past the ditched car and eased by the van which waited for them to pass.

Nancy was very still and she did not dare to speak to him. She could sense the anger in his taut body and she dreaded the 'few things' that he wished to say to her.

He did not speak until they turned from the lane into the wider road which led to the village. 'What was the idea?' he demanded harshly. 'Another scare for me?'

She shook her head mutely.

'Are you so desperate that you want to kill yourself?' he asked after a few moments.

'As if you cared!' she taunted in low tones.

'I cared enough to save your life,' he reminded her. 'If I hadn't given you a hefty shove at the right moment you'd have been under the wheels of Promise's car despite all her efforts.'

'Do you expect me to be grateful?' she asked dully.

'No. I'd have done the same for anyone,' he said cruelly. He would not admit even to himself that his heart had missed a beat as she ran full pelt towards the oncoming car and that he had put every ounce of himself into the push which saved her life, leaning low from the saddle with desperate intent.

He said nothing else until they reached her home, the old, shabby vicarage set back from the road and shaded by tall old oak trees.

CHAPTER SIX

He put his arms about her slim waist and lifted her down. He held her for a moment, steadying her – and she looked up at him with her gleaming amber eyes. He released her abruptly.

'Does your father keep anything to drink in the house?' he asked roughly.

She nodded. 'Whiskey. He likes a small glass after dinner.'

'That'll do.'

'Are you coming in?' she asked shyly. 'There's no one at home.'

He gave her a hard glance. 'What kind of an invitation is that? Social or intimate?'

Hot colour flooded her face. 'Social,' she said tautly.

He nodded. 'Okay.'

It was the first time he had been inside the vicarage and he looked about him curiously as he followed her into the quiet, peaceful house. The furnishings were shabby but hinted at good taste. She led the way into her father's study and walked across to a small cabinet which she opened. She took out a whiskey bottle and a glass and poured a generous amount into the glass. Brent studied the titles of the books in the high bookshelves. He turned as she approached and took the glass from her.

He threw back his head and drained the whiskey in one movement. 'I needed that,' he said, wiping his mouth with the back of his hand.

'Do you want another?'

'No – not now.' He took a book from the shelves and opened it. 'Your father's quite a reader. The studious type, isn't he? It's many years since I sat through one of his sermons but I remember they used to impress me when I was a kid. Where's your parents, anyway?'

'Mother has gone to visit her sister in Mellingham. Father is probably making some calls,' she explained.

'I suppose you'd better get to bed – just like the doctor ordered,' he said.

'I don't see why. I feel quite all right. My parents will think it strange if they come home to find me in bed – and I'd rather not tell them anything.'

He grinned ruefully. 'If you don't, someone else will. This place is a hotbed of gossip.'

'I'd prefer to give them my own version, if it's necessary,' she said firmly.

He looked at her steadily. 'How old are you, Nancy?'

'Nineteen. And that's the first time you've ever been interested enough to ask,' she told him quietly.

'I wasn't concerned with your age,' he said curtly. He brought the small gun from his pocket. 'Where did you get this, by the way?'

She made a move to snatch it from his hand but he evaded her adroitly. She was silent for a moment then she said: 'It belongs to my father.'

He raised an eyebrow. 'What would he want with a revolver?'

'I don't know. He's had it for years. He has a licence for it,' she added swiftly.

Deftly he opened the breech – and then he grinned. 'Well, you weren't very serious about shooting me – or didn't you know it wasn't loaded?'

She was startled. 'I never thought about it.'

He threw himself into an armchair, having placed the gun on her father's desk. He held out his hand to her. 'Come here, Nancy.'

She eyed him warily but she moved towards him. 'What do you want?'

94

He ran a hand through his hair. 'You never used to be shy of me, Nancy.' He laughed. 'What's wrong – don't you love me any more?' He regretted the mocking words as she closed her eyes briefly against a shaft of pain. He leaned forward and caught her hand firmly in his own strong fingers, drawing her towards him. 'You've made a damned fool of yourself today,' he said quietly as she stood before him. 'I hope there won't be any repeat performances.'

She caught her underlip between her teeth before she said painfully: 'I wish I'd never met you – or any of your arrogant family. The Powers think they own the world – and to hell with anyone who doesn't interest them!'

'We do own the world,' he retorted. 'So do you. So does anyone with enough sense to enjoy the world we were born into.'

'Enjoy it!' she repeated scornfully. 'Is that your explanation for the way you and your brothers behave – and your sister, too? Although Promise isn't as bad as you and Russ and Adam! You do exactly as you like – trespassing here, breaking laws there, fighting and getting drunk and waking up the village in the early hours of the morning, making love to any girl who crosses your path...'

He interrupted her. 'Not any girl, Nancy. Just the attractive ones,' he said smoothly.

'And the easy ones,' she said bitterly.

He looked at her for a long moment. 'Not necessarily. Sometimes we enjoy the triumph of a difficult conquest.'

She turned her face away. 'I wasn't difficult,' she said and there was a wealth of self-contempt in her voice.

With a firm hand under her chin, he turned her face towards him. 'You were just the way I wanted you,' he said quietly and now he was perfectly serious. 'Ardent and responsive – the kind of woman a man like me always hopes to find but seldom does. Nancy, I may be mad – in fact I know I am. I shall probably regret it for the rest of my life but I'm going to marry you.'

She was shocked by the words. Then she wrenched herself away from him. 'No! How dare you tease me so! Must you make things completely unbearable?'

He rose swiftly and caught her into his arms. 'Would it be unbearable?' he asked softly and his mouth was hard and compelling on her lips. She resisted briefly – but only briefly then he knew the warm submission of her supple body and the eager arching of her throat as her head went back and she drew him ever closer. When their lips parted, she buried her face against his shoulder.

'If only you loved me,' she whispered painfully.

He laughed. 'What do you expect – a miracle? I'll marry you. Isn't that enough for the present? Isn't it a damn sight better than marriage to a weakling like Jonothan who'd never bring his nose out of a book long enough to prove himself a man?'

'Why do you despise him so?' she protested.

He was honestly amazed. 'Despise him? Jonothan, you mean? Of course I don't despise him. I have quite an affection for him.'

Her eyes reproached him. 'That can't be true!'

'Well, it is. I may think he's something of a fool. I may think he spends too much time with his confounded books. I may scoff at him occasionally and enjoy riling him. But I'd hate you or anyone to think that I despise my own brother. He's a Power, isn't he, despite his faults. We're a very close family as you'll find out for yourself. Whatever happens, we stick together, Nancy.'

'How can I marry you? Jonothan loves me,' she said quietly.

'He told me himself that he'd rather see you married to me than anyone – if it will make you happy. Our Jonothan will enjoy the rôle of martyr, my dear, I assure you. He isn't the type of man who'll ever marry, in my opinion. I reckon he'll enjoy carrying the torch for you until the day he dies!'

She lay against his shoulder, silent and tense, while his strong hands caressed her carelessly. At last she said: 'You're not the type of man who should marry either, Brent. You'll never be faithful to me – your father told me that. You'll drink too much. You'll always be fighting. If you loved me, I could forgive all that…'

He silenced her with a rough, fiercely passionate kiss. 'Don't preach!' he said angrily. 'I'm not forcing you to marry me, am I? If you do – well, you know what to expect and you won't have any illusions for me to shatter. It's up to you, Nancy. It doesn't worry me one way or another.'

She caught her breath. His words were like a rush of cold water in her face. 'Then why did you ask me?'

'Damn you, how do I know? It's an impulse. You'd better take me up on it before I change my mind. If you'd rather have Jonothan…' He smiled slowly and kissed her deliberately, expertly, rousing the swift passion in her being as he well knew how to do. She clung to him, weak and emotional, seized in the grip of fiery, sweet passion. 'Well?' he demanded. 'You know what marriage to me will be like – you've had a foretaste of it already. Do you want to forfeit that for the meagre kind of life that Jonothan can offer?'

She shook her head. 'I want to marry you. I love you, Brent…'

Promise looked at him oddly when he entered the house. She threw aside the magazine which she had been glancing at idly. She recognised the daredevil, reckless light in his grey eyes, knew by his offhand manner that he was planning some new exploit.

'What have you been up to?' she asked suspiciously.

He grinned at her. 'Does it show?'

'I'll say it does!'

'I'm going to marry Nancy,' he said, throwing the words down like a gauntlet.

If he had hoped to surprise or dismay her, he was disappointed. She shrugged her slim shoulders. 'That's a bit tame for you, isn't it? Or do you regard marriage as a new experience which you haven't yet tried?'

'Something like that. If it doesn't work – well, I can always write finis to that chapter.'

'Nancy must be either mad or in love,' Promise said lightly. Her eyes narrowed suddenly. 'Does Jonothan know?'

He spread his hands in a deprecatory gesture. 'If he doesn't, he soon will.'

Russ came into the room at that moment. 'Where the hell did you get to?' he demanded. 'I thought you were behind me.'

Brent laughed. 'You shook me off so neatly that I decided it wouldn't be fair to spoil your fun. Was she there?'

'I don't know what you're talking about,' Russ said slowly.

'The little blonde. Sally – or whatever her name is! The girl at the *Crooked Scythe*.'

Promise broke in abruptly. 'Brent's going to marry Nancy Armstrong, Russ.'

Russ turned abruptly. 'What was that?'

Brent smiled slowly. 'You heard the lady!'

Russ grunted. 'Drunk again, I suppose. You can't have been sober to make an arrangement like that.'

'What's wrong with getting married?' Brent demanded sharply.

'Nothing, I suppose. But surely there's time enough when you've exhausted all the possibilities.'

Brent shrugged. 'I'm getting tired of taking up where other men finish. I want a woman of my own – and I'll make damn sure that no other man trespasses on my property.'

'With a girl like Nancy?' Russ sneered. He regretted the jibe as he doubled up from a hefty blow in the stomach. Groaning, he nursed his aching muscles which had been totally unprepared for the assault. 'Okay, so she's as virtuous as they come,' he said as soon as he could find his voice.

'She will be,' Brent said grimly.

Bored by the altercation, which followed similar lines to previous arguments between her brothers, Promise returned to her magazine. Russ and Brent glared at each other for a few moments – then both turned abruptly as the heavy tread of their father foretold his present entrance into the room.

He looked from one to the other suspiciously. 'Why so guilty, boys?' he asked mildly. He turned to Promise. 'Matt Nellin is coming to lunch, my dear. I've just been speaking to him on the telephone. He stayed at Mellingham last night and he isn't going back to London until this evening.'

'Why tell me?' she asked indifferently. 'I'm not interested in your protégé.'

He frowned briefly. 'Where's Adam?'

She shrugged. 'Out riding, I think.'

Russ cut in: 'He was gone before I could look round this morning. Perhaps he's gone to the Wentworth's place for lunch.'

Stephen nodded. 'He's seeing too much of that Wentworth girl. I don't like it. It's a rare thing for Adam to spend so much time with one woman. If he's thinking of settling down I'd rather he chose more wisely. Richard would be pleased, I know – but I'm damned if I can see why her expensive tastes should be paid for out of the business!'

'Brent's going to be the first one to leave the nest, Father,' Russ said with a malicious glance at his brother.

Stephen turned to look closely at Brent. 'You're a pretty sight, I must say,' he said coldly. 'By the time you're thirty you'll be as ugly as the devil if you keep up your wild ways.' He was in a bad humour, having disliked his interview with Nancy Armstrong and having heard discomfiting news from the office about a project in hand which was not running to schedule.

Brent touched his cheek idly, grinning. 'This? A foretaste of married life, Father.'

Stephen grunted. 'Didn't I tell you? That was all nonsense about Nancy having a baby. There's no need for you to marry her – or put a respectable distance between yourself and this place.'

'I'm going to marry her, anyway,' Brent said calmly.

Stephen showed no surprise. 'Please yourself, boy. I gave up worrying about your mistakes years ago. You'll have to settle the matter with Jonothan – not me!'

'He's already resigned himself to it,' Brent returned easily.

'Where is the boy, anyway?' Stephen asked, glancing about the room.

'Here, Father.' Jonothan stepped into the room from the terrace. He had been resting against the stone balustrade, watching the gardeners at work, and he had not failed to hear every word that passed in the room behind him, some of which had given him pain and others a grim amusement. He met Brent's eyes squarely. 'Congratulations Brent.' It had been a shock to learn that Nancy was not expecting his brother's child but the discovery that she had been Brent's mistress had effectively dulled his wish to marry her and he had spent a restless night suppressing the pain and disappointment and resigning himself to a life full of love for a woman he could never call his wife.

'Thanks, Jon.'

Promise called her father to her side and kept him in conversation for several minutes while the brothers talked together of various matters that held their interest.

Stephen was not very talkative and Promise was puzzled by the speculative look in his eyes. 'What are you thinking about?' she asked him with a gentle smile as he failed to answer a remark she made to him.

'Mm? Oh, nothing important,' he returned. 'Just thinking of Adam and Brent.'

She linked the connection quickly. 'You mean that you think Adam will marry Julie Wentworth?'

'It's possible, isn't it? I hate to see my son throw himself away on a worthless young woman. Everyone knows her reputation. I hoped that Adam would make a good marriage if he had to marry at all.'

'He's old enough to make his own mistakes,' she reminded him.

'I hope he realises that he'll have to pay for them,' he retorted gruffly.

Promise studied him thoughtfully, aware that he was really disturbed by the thought that Julie Wentworth might become his daughter-in-law.

'What do you think of Brent's news?'

'Nancy will do. I doubt if she'll be very happy but she has enough sense to make the most of the little she'll have from Brent. She has good blood and breeding – and I quite like the girl.'

Promise told him of the accident in the lane and her conjectures as to the cause of it. He listened in silence and then he said: 'So that's why you're home for lunch. I thought you were going to London today. I told Matt actually that you wouldn't be here.'

'I don't suppose he was disappointed,' she said coldly.

'I think he was relieved,' he said with a chuckle. He touched her shoulder briefly. 'What happened with you two in the garden, anyway? I thought you would like each other.'

She stiffened. 'It's unimportant, Father. I think it's sufficient if I say that he's completely lacking in manners and the most detestable man I ever met in my life!'

'Well, that's pretty damning,' Stephen said and his eyes twinkled. As the bell pealed throughout the house, he added: 'There he is now, I expect. Try to be reasonably pleasant to him during lunch, Promise – if only to prove that the Powers have manners at least.'

She rose to her feet and patted his cheek. 'All right, Father – to please you I'll be on my best behaviour.'

He looked apprehensive. 'Poor devil,' he said and then he laughed as she looked at him quickly.

She hurried from the room as Mathieson admitted Matt Nellin. Without a glance she began to ascend the staircase.

'Matt – this is pleasant!' she heard her father's voice boom. 'Promise! Come down here and say hello to Matt. He'll think my children have no manners.'

Muttering a curse under her breath, she turned and went down to greet him, her hand outstretched and a sweet, false smile curving her lips. He touched her fingers briefly.

'You don't look any the worse for a night of revelry,' he told her.

'Thank you, Mr Nellin,' she said, exerting all her charm but privately thinking that it was the oddest compliment she had ever received from any man.

They exchanged pleasantries while each regarded the other with veiled hostility. Then Promise excused herself prettily with a murmur of tidying her appearance before lunch.

'Don't bother on my account,' Matt said easily. 'I never notice what a woman wears, anyway, and you look all right to me.'

'I prefer to take the opinion of my mirror, Mr Nellin,' she told him smoothly and walked away from him.

She heard her father's loud laughter and his words: 'Neat, eh? She's quick with her tongue! Just like them all. And she'll do exactly as she pleases when she pleases. I'm looking forward to meeting the man who can master my daughter.'

She longed to linger to Matt's reply but sensing his eyes upon her she hurried up the wide staircase so she did not know that he turned to her father with a slow smile and a swift retort. 'We've already met, Mr Power! No woman is too rebellious or wilful for me to handle with ease!'

CHAPTER SEVEN

The meal was light-hearted and noisy. Her brothers had taken a swift liking to Matt Nellin, recognising a similar approach to life in his make-up to their own, and they regaled him with many episodes of their reckless way of life which he matched readily with stories of his own exploits in Canada and the States. Promise was silent for the most part, making a polite pretence of interest in his stories, supplying occasional encouragement, knowing that her father's eyes were upon her with approval. But it was an effort to be pleasant to the man whom she thoroughly disliked. She could not understand why her father was so impressed by his personality and she was baffled that her brothers should be so much at ease with him for she was sure that he had little time for any of them and that his contempt was ill-concealed.

He frequently met her eyes with a mocking challenge in his gaze which convinced her that he was trying to impress upon her that he was a force to reckon with and that he despised her even more than he despised her brothers. She was cool but distant throughout the meal and Stephen was well aware of the veiled hostility. He was amused but he had no intention of allowing Promise to snub Matt Nellin whom he liked, admired and respected and thought of almost in the light of a son. It did not matter whether Promise liked the man or not. Stephen was determined that she should suffer him with an outward show of courtesy and liking at least.

When they finally rose, Russ suggested that Matt might be interested in the stables and the idea was swiftly encouraged by his brother. 'We could mount you if you'd care to ride,' Brent said easily.

Matt laughed. 'Not in these clothes, thanks.'

Promise threw him a scornful glance. 'Perhaps Mr Nellin doesn't ride,' she said coolly.

He glanced at her. 'Mr Nellin worked on a ranch as a cowhand, once,' he said and the emphasis on his name was a jibe.

Russ stared. 'Is that a fact? That's something I've always wanted to do.'

'Then you should go to Canada,' Matt told him lightly.

Russ turned to his father. 'How about that? Shall I go?'

Stephen said drily: 'I don't know much about ranch life but I doubt if there's many women around.'

Matt shrugged. 'I found as many as I wanted. But it's a good life if Russ doesn't mind roughing it a bit.'

Stephen chuckled. 'My sons are not used to "roughing it" and I suspect that Russ would soon write to me for his fare back to England.' He went on: 'The only thing that appeals is the horses, believe me. None of my boys have a liking for hard work!'

Matt grinned. 'If you're any good with a horse, Russ, then you might get a job with a travelling rodeo.'

'Bucking broncos! That's an idea! Let's have a rodeo this afternoon,' Russ suggested eagerly, turning to Brent for support. 'The new stallion isn't broken in yet. How about some bareback demonstrations from you, Brent?' His brother seized on the suggestion and amid much noise, laughter and playful scuffles they made their way to the stables. Jonothan quietly slipped away on his own pursuits, unnoticed by any but Matt. Walking with Stephen, he turned to him: 'Are they really serious about this business?'

A proud little smile touched Stephen's lips. 'Sure they are! It should provide some amusement.'

'It could be dangerous, sir,' Matt objected.

Promise threw him a scornful glance. 'That's what appeals to them! You needn't worry about their necks. They've been used to horses since they were out of rompers!'

'That's true enough!' Stephen agreed. 'Danger and my boys are lifelong friends.'

Matt said no more then but a tiny frown marred his brow as Russ led out the high-spirited stallion who strongly objected to the halter rein which had been thrown about his neck. 'He looks pretty bad-tempered,' he commented.

'All the better!' Brent exclaimed cheer-fully. 'It's about time he found out that man is his master!' He took the rein from his brother's hand and stood quietly talking to the horse for a few minutes. Then, as they watched, he steadied the restive horse with a gentle hand, sliding it further up until he could grasp a strong handful of mane. Then with a swift, skilful leap he was astride the horse's back. Startled and annoyed, the horse reared but Brent kept his seat with a mighty effort. Digging his heels into the sides of the horse, leaning low over his back, he clung on, almost helpless with laughter as the angry horse tried desperately to rid himself of the annoyance. At last the horse won and Brent slithered sideways off the horse to land in a heap on the ground. With a neat roll of his powerful body, he evaded the stamping hooves and leaped to his feet.

'He's a devil!' he exclaimed as Russ moved quietly towards the stallion. 'Watch him, Russ!'

Stephen grinned and clapped his son on the shoulder. 'Not bad, eh? I'll stake a hundred that Russ keeps his seat longer than you did.' He glanced at his watch to time him, while Russ moved even closer, waiting his chance to seize the rein which the stallion was trying to cast off, pawing the ground angrily and tossing his head furiously.

Promise had been delighted by Brent's efforts and applauded him frequently as he constantly defied the frenzied attempts to unseat him. Gone was the set coldness of her features and the aloof air she had adopted with Matt throughout lunch. He glanced at her curiously, struck by the shining laughter in her eyes and the happy curve of her lips, the flush of excitement in her cheeks. She looked amazingly lovely and youthful and briefly he warmed to her although he thought she was wrong to approve her brothers' daredevil ways. However, if they chose to risk their necks, it was none of his business and he was forced to admit that Brent had proved that he knew enough about horses to look after himself. Indeed, he had been impressed by the performance.

It took Russ several minutes to get close enough to snatch the rein, longer still to quieten the stallion who regarded him warily and with a dangerous glint in his eyes.

'He's a nasty brute,' he said quietly to Promise.

She brushed aside his words. 'Russ can handle him.'

Russ proved that he could. He kept his seat with far more ease than Brent, grasping the mane with one hand and waving the other gaily as the stallion galloped about the pasture, rearing and pulling up short and then hurtling on again in the effort to unseat Russ. He let out a blood-curdling yell in mimicry of the savage Indians who had massacred many a group of pioneers making their way across uncivilised country to the West – and Matt reluctantly grinned.

He watched thoughtfully as Russ dug his heels hard into the horse and urged him to a gallop. Then, proving his mastery over the stallion, he pulled relentlessly on the rein to pull him up short a few yards from the watching group. 'Mind his mouth!' Stephen shouted in annoyance. 'Do you want to ruin him, you fool?'

Russ grinned and slid to the ground. He jerked his head at Matt. 'Come on. Show your paces, Matt. You aren't going to let Brent and I lord it over you, are you?'

Matt hesitated and would have refused regardless of the jibes which Brent and Russ were sure to throw at him. But Promise laughed scornfully. 'He doesn't want to spoil his clothes,' she called across to Russ. 'Anyway, he's afraid of Tempest. Perhaps he knows he can't handle him like that.'

Matt's lips set in a firm line. Knowing that he was a fool to accept her challenge, he strode forward, ignoring the word of cheerful encouragement which Stephen called to him and the helpful advice which Russ offered as he passed by him. Goaded by Promise's laughing words, he decided he would show them a thing or two. Familiar with horses and their various caprices, he felt no fear of the stallion and he was unconcerned that he was scarcely dressed for riding. Without bothering to quieten the horse, he took a flying leap on to his back from a standing position, knowing a moment of exultation as Promise audibly gasped and then involuntarily clapped her hands. The horse reared but he kept his seat by sheer balance and determination, scorning to grasp the mane or the rein. For a few angry, dangerous minutes Tempest did all in his power to shake Matt from his back without avail. Then Matt, determined to prove once and for all his skill with horses, began to execute a number of equestrian acrobats regardless of the stallion's dislike and rapid movements beneath him. He finished his demonstration by hanging upside down between the legs of the stallion, clinging only by his strong legs. Then he easily resumed his seat. He caught the reins and gently turned the horse towards the admiring spectators and then cantered up to them, crouching on the back and dropping easily to the ground in front of them.

There was no doubt that they were impressed and Russ, fired by the demonstration, seized the rein and leaped on to the stallion's back. The horse was tiring and almost on the point of surrendering to these humans' quaint ideas of entertainment but Russ's heel caught him painfully in the ribs and he reared unexpectedly, emitting a shrill whinny – and Russ was thrown clean over his head. He landed heavily and lay still while the horse reared again and threatened to bring his hooves down upon the man's supine body. With a swift movement, Matt was at the stallion's head, tearing at the reins, forcing him aside by sheer brute strength while Brent, Stephen and Promise ran to Russ, aghast. They scarcely noticed Matt's prompt action.

Lifting him as easily as if he had been a sack of flour, Brent picked Russ up in his arms and carried him towards the stable. Stephen and Promise hurried behind him while Matt concentrated on soothing the flurried, excited and tempestuous stallion.

When he eventually led Tempest into the stable and shut him in his stall, Russ had still not recovered consciousness and his father was looking grave. Promise was almost in tears and Brent was angry that he had encouraged his brother to indulge in such a wild and foolish escapade. Matt bent over Russ and lifted an eyelid. Then he felt his pulse. He looked up. 'I don't think there's much wrong with him. Concussed, maybe. You'd better get him up to the house and send for a doctor, anyway. I'll make myself scarce. You won't want me around.'

'Nonsense!' Stephen said roundly. 'It wasn't your fault. You tried to discourage them. I should have known better than to let them play the fool with a bad tempered brute like Tempest.'

'I don't think you can blame the horse,' Matt said quietly. 'It wouldn't be surprising if he's bad-tempered in future if he wasn't before!'

They trooped back to the house silently and a startled Mathieson was ordered to telephone for Wilson. He went off to do so, shaking his head with disapproval and it seemed to Promise as he went that he was faintly satisfied that at last he had been proved right in his prophecy that Russ would eventually come to a bad end. She caught her breath with sudden fear wondering if Russ was indeed badly hurt, perhaps too much so to live. Matt glanced at her, hearing that tiny catch of breath, and expertly read her thoughts. He had quickly realised how devoted she was to her brothers and felt sure that she was equally as proud of them as her father was. Whatever they did was certain to meet with approval in her eyes – and she had scoffed at the idea that their latest prank could be dangerous to them.

He offered her a cigarette and she took one look with a grateful gleam in her lovely eyes. 'He'll be all right,' he said confidently.

'Are you sure?' She bowed her head over the flame of his lighter. 'He looks very pale.'

'Wouldn't you after a crack on the head?' he asked. 'He's lucky he didn't break his neck outright.'

Brent joined them as he spoke. 'I think he's fractured his skull,' he said, speaking quietly. 'The old man doesn't agree with me but the way he came down it wouldn't surprise me at all.'

'It surprises me that any of you have reached your present ages,' Matt said caustically. 'You seem to delight in risking your lives.'

Brent frowned and his face took on an ugly expression. 'Does that concern you, Nellin?'

Stephen heard the threatening note in his voice and he turned abruptly. 'That's enough, Brent! I've enough on my plate this moment without you picking a quarrel with Matt.'

Brent strode to the decanters and poured a stiff whiskey for himself which he threw down in one swift movement. Inwardly he was very anxious about Russ. He also blamed himself for not heeding the dangers which attached to his brother's crazy suggestion. He ran his hands through his auburn hair.

'I think we all need a drink,' Stephen said quietly behind him and he recognised the reproof. He busied himself with supplying the others with drinks and then helped himself to another.

Promise sat beside her brother, her eyes anxious. Stephen and Brent talked in low tones while Matt stood by the window, feeling very much the outsider during this family crisis.

He was intrigued by the Powers. He knew Stephen Power well by now and both liked and admired the stocky, heavily-built man who had worked his way up from nothing to the owner of a successful concern like the Power Construction Company. He could understand the older man's love for his family but it baffled him that Stephen could be so proud of a pack of reckless young fools who did not care what happened to themselves or anyone else who became involved in their madcap exploits. Privately he considered that Stephen had always been too easy with them.

He had run into Adam several times on the occasions when he deigned to honour the offices with his company. He neither liked nor respected the man, sometimes sickened by the confidential recitals of his many adventures with women and the boastful accounts of the speaking power of his fists and brawn. Russ he knew a little better and he had great respect for his head for mathematics and his skilfulness as a designer. But he deplored his lack of interest in the company and knew sympathy for Stephen that not one of his sons showed any inclination for taking over from him in due course. He was inclined to think that Russ was the best of the bunch. He might be a woman-chaser and a fighter but he did not boast of it and he was very much a man's man. It was also possible that one day he might decide to settle down and concentrate on the business and Matt felt sure that he would prove both capable and responsible. It needed something drastic to shake him out of his wild ways and teach him that there was something more to life than women, fighting and riding.

He was a little wary of Brent. There was something more to him than ordinary wildness. He could be violent and it was more by luck than judgment that he had never yet landed a fatal blow on any of his many opponents. Matt knew that he drank too much. It was not his business whichever way Brent Power chose to make his way to his own particular hell and Matt had been known to drink a great deal himself. But he strictly disciplined himself and he had never yet lost his temper while drunk. He despised the man for making no effort whatsoever to do anything with his life but live riotously.

He had never met Jonothan until the previous evening and Stephen had failed to mention that the boy was lame. Studying him intently, Matt had decided that Jonothan was weak and over-sensitive and he was astonished that Stephen had bred such a son, so vastly different to any other member of the Power family. Stephen was proud of the boy's intelligence and had more than once spoken of his hope that Jonothan would evince an interest in the Company and perhaps prove to be the one son who could take over from him. But Matt could not visualise Jonothan in a position of such responsibility. It was evident that no amount

121

of encouragement had ever shaken him out of his retiring, studious ways or persuaded him that his lameness did not incur instinctively the pity and contempt of all who came into contact with him.

Promise. But Matt's thoughts swiftly skated away from the thought of Promise Power. He preferred not to dwell upon her evident wilfulness or the spirited temper or the mocking scorn and dislike which she had showed to him. Her beauty was undeniable – but he had known many beautiful women and she impressed him less than most. Her pride in herself as a Power was insufferable and annoyed him intensely for he firmly believed that while they might not be an ordinary family they were certainly nothing to boast about. He could think of a great many people whom he would rather have for companions than the Powers – but at the same time he was determined that Promise should not make a fool of him. She might have plenty of spirit, she might have a wicked temper, she might delight in scoring off him, she might object to his instinctive knowledge of her character – but she could do nothing to break up his close friendship with her father and she would have to put up with his occasional presence at her home. Just as he would have to put up with her brothers while he waited for an opportunity to put Promise firmly in her place. He would enjoy battling with her and his tongue could be as quick as her own. There would come a day when she would want his friendship and liking – and he would take the greatest pleasure in snubbing her without mercy...

Wilson arrived in his tiny car, resigned to yet another call at the big house and having long since grown accustomed to finding one or other of the Power boys needing his medical attention. It frequently surprised him that they escaped serious injury countless times. They healed quickly, ignored minor breakages, cuts and bruises, and were very soon going all out to need his attention again!

It took him only a few minutes to realise the gravity of Russ's condition and his eyes were sober and sympathetic as he turned to Stephen and explained that this time it would be a hospital case.

Stephen caught his arm. 'Is it serious? What's wrong with him?'

'I wouldn't like to give a definite opinion without x-rays but it's my belief that he's fractured his skull. There may be a slight injury to the spine but that's only a surmise. I shall be able to give you far more details once I can get him to Marley Hospital.'

Promise clenched her hands so fiercely that her long, well-manicured finger-nails dug deeply into her palms. For the first time in her life she knew what it meant to worry about one of her brothers in full measure.

Since childhood she had been imbued with the belief that her brothers were protected from all ills by some strange token. They had never known serious illness or injury despite their recklessness. It had always seemed to her that nothing could ever hold them down for long – but now, Wilson's quiet, noncommittal words struck a chord of fear in her heart and she turned to Brent with anxious eyes and parted lips. He glanced at her, held her gaze for a long moment and then walked from the room.

Her father consulted hastily with Wilson and then agreed that an ambulance should be sent from Marley Hospital to take Russ to the only place where he could receive expert examination and diagnosis and attention.

It was some hours later – and Matt had still not left the house – when the telephone rang and her father confirmed the fear that, her brother's skull was fractured and there was serious injury to his spine, which might or might not be permanent.

CHAPTER EIGHT

Promise slowly replaced the receiver. Then she sank into a chair. There were no tears – merely stunned dismay filling her entire being.

Matt lighted a cigarette and handed it to her. She took it listlessly and he noted the tiny crescents in her palms with the faint smears of blood staining them. He caught one of her hands and studied it. 'That was foolish,' he said quietly.

She wrenched her hand away. 'Poor Russ,' she said dully. 'Oh God, why did it have to happen to him?'

'Should it have been Brent?' he asked harshly.

She flashed him a fiery look and he was pleased, his words having been deliberately chosen to chase away the stunned expression of her eyes. 'You were playing the fool!' she accused. 'You excited Tempest.'

'Russ should have realised that the horse had become really dangerous,' he retorted. 'It was carried too far. I wish I hadn't taken him up on his challenge now.'

'It was my challenge which decided you,' she told him triumphantly.

He made no attempt to deny the truth of her words. 'I should have ignored it.' He paced the room, hands deep in his pockets. 'But I didn't – and in a way I'm entirely to blame.'

'I'm glad you realise that!' she snapped.

He turned angrily. 'Be fair, Promise! It wasn't my idea in the first place.'

'You mentioned rodeos,' she flashed.

'In casual conversation!'

'I've no intention of quarrelling with you,' she said disdainfully and stubbed the half-smoked cigarette. 'I've enough on my mind without that! My father said that Russ may never walk again...' She broke off, her face twisting with pain.

He was beside her instantly, his dislike of her and his intention to break her spirit forgotten momentarily in the realisation of her very real distress. 'Don't look like that, Promise,' he said passionately. 'It may not be true. Besides, there are specialists who'll know more about such things than country doctors like Wilson. Russ will walk again, I'm sure of it. He may be on his back for months – but he'll walk again!'

She was impressed by his vehemence and she looked at him curiously. 'Why should it matter to you?' she said flatly. 'Russ is my brother but you scarcely know him!'

'Do you think I don't feel guilty about the whole damn business?' he burst out. 'A man like Russ – to be as helpless as a baby. It doesn't bear thinking about!'

She was silent, thinking of Russ with his tall, powerful body, his amazing strength, his handsome, laughing face, his unquenchable high spirits, his prowess on a horse and his invincible lust for life. Would that body become wasted, a mockery of his former self? Would his strength be of no use to him? Would bitterness and pain distort his handsome features and drive the laughter out of his eyes for ever? Would his high spirits be for ever quenched by the realisation of his helplessness? Would he ever again mount a horse and delight those who watched him by his gay, dare-devil pranks? Would his lust for life die and leave him merely a shell of a man with interest in nothing and nobody? It did not bear thinking about, as Matt Nellin claimed, and she wondered if similar thoughts had passed swiftly through his perceptive mind.

Jonothan entered the room through the

open windows, a book in his hand and a serene expression touching his eyes. He looked from Promise to Matt – and it was obvious that he was aching to divulge something which brought that strange light to his eyes and a half-smile to his lips. He looked amazingly happy and his radiance pained Promise. She stared at him, remembering that he knew nothing of the accident which had befallen Russ for he had slipped away as they left the house to go down to the stables and nothing had been seen of him until this moment. He limped towards them – and her heart ached as she thought of the lameness he had carried with him all his life, the disability which had prevented him from enjoying life as his brothers did, the lack of strength in his slight frame – and she thought of Russ who might be for ever condemned to be even more of a cripple than his youngest brother.

Jonothan said quietly but decisively: 'I've decided to become a monk, Promise. Do you think Father will object?'

'A monk!' She was shocked. 'What put *that* into your head?'

'Oh, I don't know.' He raised the book in his hand. 'Reading the life of St Francis of Assisi, I think. I feel that the life would suit me. What do you think?'

Matt put in quietly: 'It isn't my business – but do you think you can endure hardship and poverty and all that monastery life entails? After a life of luxury and comfort, I mean?'

Jonothan looked about the room as though assessing how much happiness luxury and comfort had ever brought him. It was painful to note the brief bitterness which touched his eyes and mouth – and Matt realised that the boy had never been happy, that he had always been very much aware of the contrast between himself and his brothers and believed himself a great disappointment to his father. He did not answer Matt's question but repeated with even more decision in his voice: 'I shall become a monk.' He looked closely at Promise, noting the strain in her expression for the first time. 'Is anything wrong?' he asked quickly. 'Father...?' He stepped forward abruptly and Matt understood in that moment how much he loved and respected Stephen Power.

'Tell him,' Promise muttered, turning her face away and biting her lip against a rush of tears. She was determined that nothing would induce her to cry before Matt Nellin!

'Russ met with an accident,' Matt said quietly, addressing the boy.

Jonothan paled. 'Is he...?' He could not complete the question.

Matt finished for him: 'Dead? No. He was thrown by a horse and he's fractured his skull and injured his spine. It's possible that he may never walk again – but let's hope that isn't the case.'

Jonothan turned away and walked to the window. He stood there for a long moment without speaking. Then he said with great bitterness: 'And I was concerned with myself, my feelings and my future. I haven't given a thought to anyone but myself all afternoon – a nice, unselfish admission for a man who hopes to enter a monastery!'

'You couldn't know what had happened,' Matt said firmly. 'Don't forget that your brother Adam has been concerning himself with his own affairs all afternoon, too! We couldn't reach him to tell him what had happened.'

'Isn't he with Julie Wentworth?'

'Apparently, but her parents don't know where they've gone. Adam left his horse at their place and went off with Julie in her car. That was before lunch.'

Jonothan nodded. 'I think I know where

they are. I'll take one of the cars and go in search of Adam.'

'That isn't necessary,' Promise said quickly. 'He should be back soon. Why break bad news until we have to?'

'I'd rather be doing something,' Jonothan replied curtly and he limped from the room.

Promise shrugged. 'Let him go. He's taken it badly. It's better for him to have something else to think about – but I don't know why he should have the faintest idea where Adam and Julie could be.'

'Perhaps they frequent a certain place and Jonothan has heard Adam mention it at some time,' Matt suggested.

She nodded without much interest. Mathieson came into the room with a tray on which were set a silver coffee pot and delicate, translucent china. 'I thought you might like some coffee, Miss Promise,' he said quietly. As he set the tray on a small table beside her, he added anxiously: 'I wonder – is there any news of Master Russ yet? We're all very concerned in the kitchen, Miss Promise.'

She told him briefly and he murmured his condolences before quietly leaving the room. Promise turned to the coffee cups. 'No doubt Peggy and Molly are crying their eyes out,' she said caustically. As Matt glanced at her with raised brows, she added: 'The maids. He flirts outrageously with them both and they think he's wonderful. Servants love an excuse to cry into their never-ending supply of tea-cups.'

He took the cup she offered to him. 'Thanks,' he said absently. 'Hasn't he a regular girl? Someone who should be told, I mean?'

She laughed grimly. 'Russ? Who knows? I'm sure I wouldn't know. He always has several girls in tow.' The shrilling of the telephone caused her to look up from the coffee pot. 'The hospital?' she asked with held breath.

Matt shrugged. 'I shouldn't think so.'

Mathieson hovered in the doorway. 'It's a young lady enquiring for Master Russ,' he said discreetly. 'Shall I...?'

'Put it through. I'll speak to her,' Matt told him decisively and ignored the indignant glance which Promise directed at him. As soon as Mathieson closed the door she turned on him.

'When did you decide to give orders in this house?' she demanded coldly.

'Two minutes ago,' he returned calmly. 'If this is one of Russ's girl-friends, it's better

133

for me to speak to her. She'll think I'm one of your brothers. Don't you agree that she might be embarrassed talking to a member of her own sex? Wouldn't you be?' He lifted the receiver. 'Hallo? Can I help you?'

'I want to speak to Russ. Is he there?' The girl's voice sounded breathless and uncertain.

'Not at the moment, I'm afraid. Can I give him a message?'

'Oh, do you think he's left to meet me? I'm Sally – Sally Whitlock! He promised to meet me this evening and I've waited and waited. Perhaps I shouldn't have rung up...' Her voice trailed off in apprehension.

He covered the mouthpiece. 'Sally Whitlock,' he said quietly to Promise. 'Know her?'

She nodded. 'The daughter of the man who keeps the *Crooked Scythe*. Surely she doesn't know Russ well enough to telephone him?' Her tone was aloof, faintly tainted with snobbery. His glance was reproachful but he made no reply, turning back to the telephone.

'Sorry about that. Someone spoke to me. Look here, I'm sorry you've been kept waiting but I'm afraid Russ met with an accident this afternoon.' He heard the swift intake of breath.

'Is he hurt?'

'I'm afraid so. He's at Marley Hospital right now.'

'Oh no! Would they let me see him? It *is* important!'

He hesitated. Then he said regretfully: 'No, I don't think they would, Miss Whitlock. Not tonight, anyway. But try not to worry.' He heard a vaguely familiar sound and he said quickly: 'I say, don't cry, Sally. Look, where are you?'

'Where he said he'd meet me – at the crossroads,' came the muffled reply.

'Well, you come up to the house and I'll explain it all to you,' he said warmly.

'Oh, I can't do that!' she exclaimed, startled.

'Of course you can. I'm sure Russ would want you to know what happened.'

'Didn't he *say* that he was supposed to meet me?' she wanted to know shyly.

'Well, I'm afraid he didn't. But I guess he didn't feel much like talking. You get here as quickly as you can – we'll keep the coffee pot warm for you,' he told her and a faint smile touched his lips.

Promise did not interrupt but she was seething at his high-handed invitation to the girl. As he put down the receiver she snapped: 'She won't come! You were wasting your breath!'

'Why won't she come?' he demanded.

She shrugged. 'Because she knows her place. She may be quite friendly with Russ but she's never been to this house – and she knows better than to come uninvited.'

'I've just invited her,' he reminded her grimly.

'By what right?' she demanded, indignant. 'This is not your house, Mr Nellin.'

He grinned, unperturbed by her indignation. 'I know that but the girl was upset and anxious. I know as little as you do about her relationship to Russ – but I feel damn sure that she's entitled to know why he couldn't keep their appointment.'

'What makes you so sure that he meant to keep it, anyway? He's always dating village girls and then failing to turn up.'

He rubbed his chin thoughtfully. 'I guess I have a feeling that this is one girl he didn't mean to fail. You may be as snobbish as you like, Promise – but I mean to give the girl a cup of coffee and a warm welcome. Do you think I give a damn whether she's a publican's daughter? And I fail to see why you should with your lack of pedigree,' he added and it was a sneer.

She stiffened. 'What do you mean by that? My mother was the daughter of a wealthy baronet!'

'And your father was the son of a labourer and a kitchen-maid,' he told her grimly. 'You and your brothers have more of that blood than any handed down by your well-born mother, if you ask me!'

She was on her feet instantly, pale with temper, her eyes blazing. 'How dare you insult my father?'

He laughed. 'Insult him! He's probably proud of the fact.'

'I don't believe you,' she stated with a dangerous glint in her eyes.

He raised an eyebrow. 'Then your old man has never mentioned it to you. A pity! It might have kept you from turning into a snob and being so full of your own importance. Well, my dear Promise, I had it from the lips of your father himself – why don't you ask him yourself?'

Forced to believe him yet wishing she could prove him a liar, she fell back on his easy use of her given name which she resented so much. 'I can't remember that I ever gave you permission to call me Promise,' she threw at him. 'I'm Miss Power to you – please don't forget it!'

'Oh, come off your high horse,' he said lightly. 'Your father doesn't object if I call him Steve at the office – why should you mind familiarity?'

'Because it's particularly objectionable coming from you!' she told him coldly.

He shrugged. 'I'm pretty objectionable all round in your eyes, I guess. But I'd hate you to think that it worries me. My opinion of *you* isn't particularly high, as a matter of fact.'

'I'm not interested in your opinion of me or anything else,' she retorted, tilting her chin proudly. 'If you had any common decency, you'd have taken yourself off hours ago. I'm sure I didn't ask you to stay around and make a nuisance of yourself!'

His lips tightened. 'Your father asked me if I would wait here until he came home. Believe me, it isn't my choice. I can think of far better ways to spend my time than keeping a spoiled brat company.'

She flushed angrily. 'I think you're extremely rude,' she said, rising to her feet. 'At least I don't have to entertain you. Or any of Russ's common girl friends!'

His eyes held great contempt. 'My manners may not be so great but you haven't any at all. Suit yourself if you stay or not. It would be too much to hope that you could be polite at least to Sally Whitlock.'

She walked towards the door, disdaining to reply, infuriated by the man who watched her progress across the room with nothing but loathing and contempt in his gaze. She had never lacked for male admiration and it was perhaps the first time in her life that anyone had shown their dislike of her so openly. It was a blow to her pride and vanity that Matt Nellin was totally unimpressed either by her looks, her personality or the fact that she was a Power. Not that she cared for his opinion one way or the other, she assured herself firmly, but in the same moment she thought of his easy friendliness and forceful, distinctive manner which had undeniably impressed her on the night of her birthday ball. He was no longer friendly towards her. She had antagonised him once and for all by her swift repulsion of his advances. She did not care for that but it seemed a pity that she could not now attempt to intrigue his interest and then flaunt him as her latest conquest. For he was handsome and attractive and that wicked, mocking glint in his dark eyes could weaken her firm resolution to snub him mercilessly.

He seemed immune to snubs and was quite ill-mannered enough to return them and match her fiery vehemence with his own when he chose.

Her hand on the panel of the door, she paused. It might be amusing to change her attitude to him, to persuade him that she was after all a sweet, lovely and desirable woman, to ensnare him firmly in the meshes of her net – and then treat him with cold contempt and teach him that it was both foolish and presumptuous of him to imagine for a moment that she was seriously interested in him as a man!

She turned abruptly and flashed him her loveliest, warmest smile which held a cleverly calculated hint of rueful contrition. 'Shall we cry pax?' she asked, holding out her hand. 'It seems so silly to quarrel when my father is obviously so keen that we should be friends.'

He looked at her suspiciously then he stepped forward and took her hand. 'I wonder if you mean to heal the breach – or if it's merely a ruse for reasons of your own,' he said, clasping her slim fingers firmly and gazing down at her, searching her eyes.

She allowed her hand to rest in his and pouted prettily. 'How unkind of you to misjudge me!'

He laughed coolly. 'I'm not unintelligent, you know – and this surprising *volte face* on your part rouses my suspicions. Are you hoping I might change my mind about you and give you every opportunity to make a fool of me?'

She opened her eyes wide in innocence. 'I don't understand you, Matt.'

'So it's to be first names, after all?' His eyes mocked her. 'I think you'd better find someone greener than me to play tricks on, Promise. I'm not likely to alter my opinion of you – and I might as well tell you right now that you might be clever enough to bamboozle quite a few men but nothing you think up will persuade me that you're anything but a tempting, immoral witch with a liking for men and absolutely no scruples!'

She snatched her hand away and raised it to strike him, pale and trembling with anger, bereft of words in the shock of realising that he had skilfully and truthfully read her thoughts.

He caught her wrist in a fierce, painful grip and drew her close. 'I advise you not to struggle,' he said grimly. 'I might break your wrist!' She pounded him with her free hand but he merely laughed mockingly as she made no impression on his muscular, hard chest. 'Save your energy,' he told her. 'One of these days you'll find out that it's fatal to strike me. Do it again – and I shall take the greatest pleasure in returning the compliment!'

'You wouldn't dare!'

'Try me and see,' he suggested, his eyes glinting dangerously.

She ceased to struggle and stood rigid, her bearing icy, her anger beyond control. 'Please let me go!' She ground through her teeth. He held her tighter and bent his head. Realising his intention, she swiftly averted her face. 'Kiss me – and I'll bite you till the blood flows,' she threatened.

He thrust her away, so abruptly that she staggered and almost fell. 'I'd rather kiss a raging tiger than you!'

She was almost frightened by the look in his eyes and without a word, nursing her bruised wrist, she hurried from the room.

Matt pulled out a pack of cigarettes and thrust one between his lips. He was almost trembling – partly with anger, partly because the flood of passion she had aroused in him had not yet ebbed away. He was a fool to give her a second thought. She was all that he disliked in a woman – wilful, tempestuous, cold and disdainful, deceitful and cunning, proud and arrogant and vain. But despite all these faults he was determined that she would realise one day her folly in antagonising him. It would be very easy to keep away from her and dismiss her completely from his mind. But he was too proud to allow any woman to defeat him – and Promise Power was not going to be the first to do so. He would crush her will and humble her pride. He would tear away her arrogance and vanity. He would match cunning with cunning. He would melt that cold heart and break that tempestuous spirit no matter what it cost him!

So determined, he turned a quelling face towards the young girl who hesitated shyly on the threshold of the room and she was filled with apprehension – but then he smiled, that warm, charming smile, and moved towards her eagerly.

CHAPTER NINE

Sally Whitlock was younger than he had expected although he had guessed from her lack of composure on the telephone that she was youthful and unsure of herself. Her small, piquant face was flushed and apprehensive and her blue eyes were dark with fear. But her expression cleared as he greeted her warmly, bade her sit down and turned to the coffee pot.

'Don't look so worried, Sally,' he said kindly. 'Russ is very ill but I'm sure he's going to be all right.'

She looked at him curiously. 'I thought you were one of his brothers when you talked to me on the telephone.'

He smiled. 'I should have introduced myself before. My name is Matt Nellin. I'm a friend of the family.'

Her eyes brightened. 'Russ mentioned you today. I remember now.'

'You've seen him today? Was that when he arranged to meet you this evening?'

'Yes. He rode over this morning.' She

flushed a little. 'My father keeps a pub a few miles away. I've seen Russ there several times.'

He handed her a cup of coffee and offered cigarettes. She refused a cigarette and he smiled down at her. 'You're fond of Russ?'

She nodded. 'Yes, I am.'

He liked the direct, candid reply. 'You know him well by now, I suppose.'

She met his eyes squarely. 'Not as well as you may imagine. I know he has a reputation with women – but it's different this time. He's never tried to make *me* do anything wrong.'

He was rather touched by her naïve explanation and studying the youthful simplicity of expression, the purity of her blue eyes and the natural dignity of her bearing, he knew an instinctive respect for her – and then he understood why Russ had treated her differently to his other women friends. Briefly he wondered at the extent of interest Russ felt for Sally Whitlock but before he could phrase a discreet question she spoke again.

'Russ says that he wants to marry me. I know it isn't sensible and I've told him time and again that I can't marry him.'

He sat down beside her on the settee and

stretched his long legs, perfectly at ease with the simple, country girl. 'Why not? You love him, don't you?'

'Oh yes! But he's the son of Stephen Power – and my father's a publican. Not that there's anything wrong in that,' she added hastily, 'but Russ and I – well, we have different roots, Mr Nellin, and it wouldn't work out. He ought to marry someone rich and beautiful who wouldn't shame him.'

'What about you?'

She shrugged. It was an odd little shrug, eloquent of her lack of concern for herself. 'It wouldn't matter to anyone if I never married, would it? My Dad would be disappointed and naturally my mother thinks it would be a great thing for me to marry Russ. They don't understand. If I ever did get married it would have to be to someone like me – plain and ordinary without any money or wealthy friends and a taste for extravagant living.'

Matt privately thought that if Russ seriously wanted to marry Sally Whitlock then he should do so, for it would be the best thing for him to have a wife without an ounce of false pride in her entire being and who could do more than anyone else in making something worthwhile of him but he was perceptive and understanding enough to appreciate her point of view. 'You'd have to love Russ a great deal to marry him,' he said quietly. 'He wouldn't be an easy husband to live with.'

She was quick in her defence. 'It isn't his fault that he's always been allowed to do as he likes and has had ample money to make his life easy. I know him, Mr Nellin. I know he has a quick temper and that several men have suffered for it. I know he's wild and restless by nature. But I blame his father and brothers for that! Mr Power should have brought him up more strictly. As for Adam and Brent...' She spoke with a trace of contempt. 'Brent's always the first to start a fight and Adam hasn't the faintest idea of setting a good example.' Suddenly she coloured and glanced at him uncertainly. 'Perhaps I shouldn't be talking like this to you, Mr Nellin. I mean ... well, you're one of their friends...'

He smiled reassuringly. 'Not one of the rich and pleasure-loving friends, believe me. You can say just what you like to me, Sally – and I wish you'd call me Matt. I feel old enough to be your father when you call me Mr Nellin!' He was glad that a slight chuckle broke from her. He was even more glad that Promise had flounced from the room in a huff. Sally Whitlock would not have dared to talk to him if Promise had been present and he felt certain that Promise would have shrivelled the child in no time with a frigid glance and a few disdainful words.

She was silent for a moment. Then she went on: 'I believe Russ would be quite happy if he didn't have much money – as long as he could have a horse of his own. He plays the fool with his brothers because they'd laugh at him if he didn't. But really, Mr ... Matt, he's *quite* different with me!' she finished earnestly having stumbled on his name but manfully fallen in with his wishes.

'Yes, I can believe that,' Matt said soberly. He quietly told her of the wild escapade which had brought about the fall and Russ's sojourn in hospital. She listened without interruption but her face was pale and her eyes, steadily fixed on him, darkened as he explained that the man she loved might never walk again and could not be relied on to survive his fractured skull.

She did not speak when he stopped talking and he waited patiently while she struggled for composure. He was convinced that if Russ lived the best thing for him would be to marry this young, sweet girl with her innate common sense. He did not doubt for a moment that she could be persuaded to marry Russ. She would not be concerned with his helplessness but only with her lack of breeding and background which seemed to her to be such a stumbling-block in the way of a future with Russ.

He said quietly: 'You know Russ is going to need you more than ever now.' She was startled and proved it by the swift turn of her head. 'He's going to hate being confined to bed for an indefinite length of time. If it's true that he can't walk again, he's going to go through hell. If he asked you to marry him then he must love you – and if you really care enough for Russ, then you'll realise that you should marry him as soon as he's well again. In the meantime, try to see him as much as possible and whatever happens, don't let him talk you out of marrying him. For the Powers are damnably proud, aren't they?' He smiled at her. 'He's likely to tell you that if you wouldn't marry him when he was well and active, he's damned if he's going to allow you to tie yourself to a helpless cripple!' He did not stress the possibility of death which attached to Russ Power's condition. It seemed to him that she had enough to cope with.

'You're so kind,' she said softly. 'I don't know how to thank you! I realise now that I should never have refused Russ in the first place. He does need me – and he always did! It doesn't really matter to anyone who or what I am, does it?'

He shook his head. 'Only to you and Russ – and need it make any difference? Stephen Power may be a wealthy man – but he wasn't born to it although that may not be common knowledge.'

She turned an eager face to him. 'Is that true?'

'It certainly is – so you can discard all thoughts of your not being good enough for Russ, my dear.'

'When do you think I'll be able to see him?' she asked anxiously.

He pulled thoughtfully. 'I can't tell you, Sally. But I'll try to pull a few strings for you through Mr Power.' The sound of an approaching car caught his attention and he glanced towards the open window. 'I should think that's Mr Power now, back from the hospital.'

She rose hastily. 'I'd better not meet him

now. Can I slip through the window and go home across the stream?'

He laid a detaining hand on her arm. 'He's no ogre, I assure you. Besides, you must know him.'

'Only slightly,' she said apprehensively. 'I don't suppose I've ever spoken to him. Please, Matt – I'd really rather not see him now.'

'My dear child, how can you expect me to ask him to help you see Russ if he doesn't know who the devil I'm talking about,' he said quietly and sensibly.

Stephen came heavily into the room. He was tired and anxious and he looked several years older in that moment. He greeted Matt and nodded without interest to Sally, scarcely noticing her. Brent followed him into the room and looked with some amazement at the young girl. But he had always treated her with friendly ease and he said now: 'Hallo, Sally. You're quick off the mark. Come to find out how Russ is, have you?'

Stephen turned from the decanters. 'Russ? He's in a bad way, there's no doubt of it. Kind of you to enquire, m'dear.' His kindly tone, combined with the sorrowful way in which he spoke of Russ, brought swift, painful tears to her eyes and he stared at her sharply. 'There, there! Don't cry, lass,' he said awkwardly. 'It could be worse, couldn't it?'

Matt tightened his grip on Sally's arm. 'I'm glad you got back before Sally went home. Russ had arranged to meet her and she telephoned to find out why he didn't turn up. I suggested she should come to the house and have some coffee with me while we waited for you and Brent to get back, Steve.'

Stephen looked at him sharply, aware of the appeal in the familiar use of his first name which had been formerly preserved for the intimacy of his office. He glanced through lowered brows at the girl, wondering why Matt had judged it so important that she should wait for his return.

Sally said shyly: 'Perhaps I shouldn't have come, Mr Power. But I was so anxious about Russ.'

Her gentle, sweet voice and the lack of fear for him impressed Stephen and he allowed a glimmer of a smile to break through the grimness of his expression. 'Any friend of my son is welcome here, m'dear.' There was a note of curiosity in his voice.

Brent said idly: 'It's Sally Whitlock, Father.

From the *Crooked Scythe*. You must have heard us mention her. Anyway, you know her old man well enough.'

Stephen looked more intently at Sally. 'Good lord! Of course I know you, child. How you've grown! You were knee high to a grasshopper the last time I noticed you. I didn't think you were old enough to interest any of my sons.' His eyes narrowed suspiciously. 'Very friendly with Russ, are you, eh?'

She glanced swiftly at Matt for guidance and he said smoothly: 'Friendly enough to become your daughter-in-law, Steve.'

Brent spun round from the window where he had been standing, nursing a glass of whiskey, and idly watching the evening sunset. 'What's that! It's the first I've heard of such an arrangement!'

'Or anyone else,' grunted Stephen. He ran a hand around the back of his neck to ease the slight stiffness and dull ache. 'I've had enough surprises for one day, I think. What with your engagement to Nancy Armstrong – and Russ putting himself in a hospital bed! The next thing will be Promise wanting to get married, I suppose?'

'No, Father,' Promise said lightly from the doorway. 'You're wrong there. I'm afraid it's

Jonothan who has a surprise in store for you.'

'Jonothan!' Stephen repeated, startled. 'Why? What crackpot scheme has he evolved now?'

'He wants to be a monk!' Promise announced with a light laugh.

Stephen groaned. 'Marriage yesterday – a monastery today. The devil take you all! Go your own ways – and be damned to you!' He stumped from the room, muttering under his breath.

Promise and Sally looked at each other steadily: the one with cool hostility; the other with a natural, calm dignity and resolution which forced Promise to drop her gaze. 'What makes you think that Russ wants to marry *you?*' she asked coldly.

Sally lifted her head. 'Why don't you ask Russ how many times he's proposed to me?'

Matt broke in hastily: 'Now then, girls! Is this the time for petty discourtesies with Russ unable to speak for himself in the matter? Why don't we all have a drink and be friends? Then I'll walk home with Sally.'

Promise shrugged and turned to Brent, enquiring after Russ. Brother and sister talked in low tones while Matt tried to persuade Sally to have a drink. Failing, he smiled down at her and repeated the suggestion that he should walk home with her which she gratefully accepted.

As soon as they were alone, Promise turned from the window, having watched them walk away from the house with an ugly look in her eyes. 'Can you tell me why Father is so taken with that loathsome creature?' she demanded of Brent angrily.

He raised an eyebrow. 'Sally? She's all right. Quite a nice kid...'

She interrupted him patiently. 'I'm talking of Matt Nellin!'

He grinned. 'Why don't you like him? I should have thought he was just the type to appeal to you, Promise.'

'Well, he doesn't. I dislike him intensely and I shall be glad when he leaves us in peace.'

He took little notice of her words. 'You know, the old man is right. This has been quite a day.' He stretched his powerful body, drawing himself to his full height and yawning. 'I shall welcome the dinner gong. I think I'll bath and change then I'll be ready to go down to the village.'

She eyed him scornfully. 'You're not meeting Nancy tonight?'

'Why not? Because of Russ. Sitting around

155

worrying about him won't help and he'd be the first one to urge me to enjoy myself. And that's just what I intend to do.'

'You're callous!' she threw at him.

'Maybe. But if you had a date you wouldn't break it because of Russ, either,' he taunted her.

She turned her back on him. He sauntered from the room, whistling merrily, much to her disgust. She was angry because he had been, as usual, annoyingly blunt and she was forced to admit that there was more than a grain of truth in his words.

A little of her anger was directed against Matt Nellin who had been busily exerting his charm on that stupid girl who was little more than an impressionable child. She was unimpressed by the announcement that Sally was hoping to marry Russ. For one thing, she strongly doubted that Russ could have any intention other than making the girl his mistress. For another, though it might be true, she felt it was scarcely an opportune moment for the girl to claim that she was engaged to Russ. She wondered why Matt had been so obviously attracted by the girl's cloying personality and lack of intelligence.

Stephen Power came into the room.

'Promise, don't you want your dinner? The gong sounded a few minutes ago.'

She went over to him. 'I'm sorry if I kept you waiting, Father. I didn't hear it.'

He patted her hand. 'Thinking about Russ, are you? Try not to worry, my dear. Wilson was a little more hopeful when we left the hospital. At least it seems likely that he'll live – and we couldn't be sure of that a few hours ago, could we?' He glanced around the room with a trace of surprise. 'Why, where's Matt?'

'He's walked home with Sally Whitlock,' she answered briefly.

He frowned. 'But isn't he staying for dinner. I thought we might suggest he spent the night here, Promise. He could travel to Town with me in the morning. What do you think?'

'I wish you wouldn't, Father,' she said with a note of pleading in her voice. 'He is a stranger, after all, and I'm sure he feels uncomfortable knowing that we're too concerned for Russ to show more than ordinary politeness at the moment.'

'Oh, Matt won't care for that,' he said stoutly. 'He'd prefer to be regarded as one of the family. No need for ceremony with Matt, you know.'

The only ceremony she liked to think of in connection with Matt Nellin was purely sacrificial, she told herself with savage humour. But she made no reply, linking her hand in her father's arm and walking from the room with him.

'This nonsense of Jonothan's? Does he mean it?' Stephen asked abruptly.

She shrugged. 'I'm sure I don't know, Father. It may be just a passing idea but I must say he was absolutely radiant when he told us about it. Perhaps he is cut out for that kind of life. He's certainly the "odd one out" in this family.'

He pursed his lips thoughtfully. 'Where is the boy, anyway?'

'He dashed off to find Adam. We telephoned the Wentworths but Adam and Julie had gone off somewhere in her car. Jonothan reckoned that he knew where they would be so he went in search of them to break the news and bring Adam back as quickly as possible.'

He grunted. 'I don't like it,' he muttered as they entered the long, panelled dining-room.

'What, Father?'

'Adam and Julie Wentworth. I've nothing to say about the other affairs. But I can't stomach the thought of my eldest son choosing a wife like that. She's had affairs with more men than I care to remember. Bad blood in her, don't care what you say. She's not for Adam if I can prevent it.' He pulled out a chair for her and then took his own seat. 'Young, irresponsible fool!' he growled.

Brent, already seated, glanced up from his plate. 'You know Adam will do exactly as he chooses, Father. You've always encouraged us in that line so if he marries a girl you disapprove of, you must blame yourself for being so lax with us all.'

'Easy to say that, isn't it? With you making a hash of your own life!' Stephen said swiftly, his quick temper aroused. 'There's Jonothan talking of being a monk – and Matt telling me that old Whitlock's daughter wants to marry Russ and he's willing enough. I'm beginning to think that Promise is the only one of you with any sense!'

His daughter smiled serenely at her discomfited brother who returned no reply but attacked the food on his plate with a vicious look on his face.

'There must be something in the air lately,' Stephen went on hotly. 'Everything's happening too quickly for my liking.' He toyed aimlessly with his food.

Promise laughed lightly and laid her hand on her father's stocky wrist. 'Powers are noted for their fast pace, Father. Is it so surprising that your sons should attack their love affairs with speed and gusto?'

Slightly mollified, he patted her hand and twinkled at her beneath bushy eyebrows. 'The sooner they're off my hands the better, eh? Perhaps you're right, Promise – perhaps you're right. I've done all I can for them. It's time they assumed some responsibilities and a wife is the toughest of them all!' He chuckled at his own joke but the sound was more grim than light-hearted.

CHAPTER TEN

Promise tossed her gloves and jaunty little hat on to the desk and walked to the window. She looked down on the busy street below and watched the hurrying pedestrians for a few moments, idly thinking that they looked like ants so far below.

Her father's office and adjoining town flat were situated at the top of the high block which contained the busy offices of the Power Construction Company. Whenever Promise had occasion to visit the building she always felt the thrill of pride and admiration for her father's name and reputation as a businessman that she knew now as she turned from the window.

She helped herself to a cigarette from the ebony box which lay on his desk and sat down in the comfortable, leather armchair, crossing one leg elegantly over the other. Her fashionably short skirt rode up to reveal slim, nylon shod knees. The dress she wore was a simple black affair relieved only by a string of exquisite pearls and a pearl cluster brooch at waist level. It had been an extravagant buy but she did not regret it. Idly she glanced through the papers that lay on her father's desk but there was little to interest her among them.

Her newly-shampooed hair gleamed brightly in the sunshine and her grey eyes danced with merriment as she thought of her father's surprise when he returned to his office. She seldom bothered to visit him when she was in London for her days were usually packed with social engagements or visits to the hairdressers or shopping expeditions. But, finding herself at a loose end, she had decided to suggest that her father take her out to lunch.

Her father's secretary had informed her that he had gone to another office to discuss details of a new project but that if Miss Power cared to wait she would try to locate him and advise him of her presence in his office.

Suddenly the door opened and Promise leaped up, expecting her father, a warm and loving smile illumining her beautiful features. The smile vanished abruptly and she looked with ill-concealed annoyance into Matt Nellin's dark eyes.

He nodded to her. 'We meet again.'

'Didn't Miss Framley tell you that my father was not in his office?' she demanded coldly.

'Naturally. I wanted to leave some papers for him. She mentioned that you were here – but I can assure you it didn't make me change my mind. Why are we so honoured by your presence?' he asked with cool sarcasm.

'It's none of your business but I decided to lunch with my father. Any objections?'

'One very important one. Your father has an appointment for lunch and he isn't likely to break it just to please a whim of yours.'

Her face fell. 'An appointment?'

'Why does that surprise you? He doesn't usually eat alone.' He did not look at her as he gave one last glance through the papers in his hand before placing them on the desk. 'Don't look so downcast. I'm free for lunch. I'll be ready in ten minutes.' He went from the room swiftly, leaving her so abruptly that she had no time to refuse.

She laughed mockingly. So he would take her to lunch. Well, she knew just the place – and she meant to eat a really hearty meal. That would damage his pocket and make him think twice about taking her out to lunch – or anywhere else for that matter. His studied indifference had piqued her, for she was unaccustomed to such casual manners and such an easy acceptance of her presence.

When her father came in, she greeted him warmly but absently. He looked at her closely. 'What's on your mind, Promise?' he asked, knowing her well.

She shrugged. 'Nothing. I slipped in to see you for a few minutes.'

'Want me to take you to lunch, I suppose? I guessed as much. Sorry, my dear, it's impossible today. But I've told Matt to take you and assured him that I'll foot the bill.'

Angry, she stared at him. 'You *told* Matt Nellin to take me to lunch?'

'Yes. He wasn't very keen but he'll do anything for me,' he replied absently, picking up the papers that Matt had left for him.

'How kind of him,' she said icily, dangerously.

'He's quite a fine person when you get to know him,' he agreed, failing to notice the icy tone and the dangerous glint in her eye. He looked up and his eyes twinkled. 'His lip healed all right, my dear. I don't know if his pride did the same. It's my guess that he isn't usually rebuffed by attractive women, what do you think?'

'I'm not particularly interested,' she said haughtily.

He chuckled. 'That means you are. Good! He'd make you an excellent husband, Promise.'

'Have you also decided how many children we should have?' she demanded furiously.

He met her eyes levelly, his own wide with innocence. 'Surely that's out of my province, my dear. You must discuss that with Matt when you marry him.'

'Marrying Matt is about as unlikely as … as…' She broke off, unable to think of any comparison that would be scathing enough.

'As me knocking Brent cold, eh?' he asked with a dry laugh. 'Nevertheless it happened – and it surprised me as much as him, believe me!'

She tossed her head and walked to the door. 'When Mr Nellin arrives, tell him that I prefer to choose my own friends, will you?' she asked haughtily as the door opened and Matt hesitated on the threshold, a mocking gleam in his eyes.

Her glance was scornful and she would have brushed by him but he detained her with a hand on her arm. 'I might be late back, Mr Power,' he said lightly. 'All right by you?'

'Of course, my boy. Take as long as you like. I know Promise likes to linger over a meal.' He nodded to them both affably. 'Enjoy yourself, my dear,' he said to Promise.

Outside the closed door, she wrenched her arm away and only the curious glance of Miss Framley prevented her from speaking her mind there and then. She bestowed a polite, charming but frigid smile on the secretary and stalked from the outer office. Matt winked at the girl and followed Promise on to the thickly-carpeted landing. He pressed the button which brought the lift and turned his head to smile at Promise.

'I've reserved a table at the Cosmo-politan,' he said. 'Your father said it was one of your *favourite* places.'

'You shouldn't have bothered,' she told him coldly although she was impressed by his forethought. 'I'm not in the least hungry and I don't think I'll stay in Town for lunch. I can always stop for something on the way home.'

'Don't be childish,' he reproved her mildly. 'Do you think it pleases me to take a woman out by order of her father? I like to choose my own friends, too. Or hasn't that occurred to you?'

She was annoyed that he had overheard her words to her father and she stepped into the lift without a reply. They were carried down to ground level and she turned towards her long, white sports car as they left the building. He shook his head. 'We'll take a taxi. You won't find a place to park that monstrosity anywhere in the West End at this time of the day.'

She tightened her lips but followed him to the taxi which had miraculously appeared as he spoke and pulled up at the slight lift of his hand. Knowing how difficult it was to obtain an empty taxi at the busiest hour of the day, she was again impressed but she was determined that she would not show it.

In the taxi, he leaned against the leather seat and closed his eyes. Promise studied him with reflective eyes. They had not met since the fateful week-end of her birthday ball and Russ's accident. He was undeniably attractive… It was a pity that he was not also likeable. He looked a rogue, she decided – and wondered why that should please her. She had no personal interest in Matt Nellin. Indeed, he aroused no feeling but one of animosity where she was concerned.

'You look tired,' she said.

He opened his eyes. 'I was up half the night working,' he replied absently.

'Working?' There was a mocking note of disbelief behind the word.

'What do you think? Womanising? My name isn't Power,' he said drily.

Anger swept through her. 'What do you mean?'

'Oh, come off that high horse,' he said wearily. 'The only one with any morals in your family is your father – and Jonothan, perhaps. He's a nice kid. It's a pity he's lumbered with your brothers' reputation because of his name. Is he still determined to become a monk?'

She ignored the question. 'I'm not interested in your opinions. Our morals scarcely concern you, anyway!'

'They concern your old man and you're making him an old man between you, too! He looks drawn and anxious these days and you can't blame it all on Russ. Why the hell can't you all stop being parasites and make a life of your own? Give the poor devil some peace!'

'Are those my father's sentiments or yours?' she asked with deceptive sweetness.

'Mine, of course.'

'Then mind your own business!' she snapped. 'If my father once heard your impertinent remarks you'd be out of a job,' she added in conversational tones.

He smiled. 'I doubt it. He depends on me too much. God knows he needs someone he can rely on.'

'Perhaps I should learn to type and take the place of his secretary,' she suggested caustically.

'That's not a bad idea, either,' he retorted. 'It would be more worthwhile than racketing about the countryside doing damn all!'

She withdrew into herself, hurt by his criticism no matter how well-founded it might be, and resenting his outspokenness in affairs that did not concern him.

Within a few minutes, they reached the restaurant and he helped her from the taxi, paid the driver and escorted her through the swing doors into the elegant foyer. Idly, Promise wondered how he would carry himself in a smartly expensive habitué of the wealthy and idle socialites. If she had hoped that he would be ill at ease, he disappointed her. He knew his way around and again she was faintly impressed by his ease of manner. For the first time, she wondered about his background. All she knew of him was that he was a Canadian. She had never been interested enough before to learn more and he was something of a mystery man.

They entered the elegant Cocktail Bar with its stimulating, sophisticated décor. As they sipped cocktails, he looked about him, grimacing. 'I can't say I care for this place,' he said bluntly. 'Too many of the wrong types.'

She smiled at him sweetly. 'I'm one of them, of course.'

He studied her intently, weighing her words. 'Not really,' he said after a brief silence. 'There's a lot of good qualities going to waste behind that stupid veneer of sophistication. Why don't you drop the pose and be yourself, Promise?'

'I am myself,' she said with a light laugh. 'I'm sorry if you don't care for my personality but there's nothing false about it!'

'You're natural enough with me,' he retorted. 'But that's because I don't allow you to be anything else. I rile you too much and then you really let yourself go. It's my guess that not many of your men-friends know what a bad-tempered, bad-mannered and ill-behaved little madam you are. Or do you fail to deceive everyone with your sweetness and charm and air of pretty manners?'

She flushed. 'Considering that we're almost strangers you presume to know a great deal about me!' she threw at him.

He grinned. 'We almost lived in each other's pockets that week-end. How can we be strangers? I soon summed you up, if that's what you mean. You put on a pretty act for me but it soon dropped when I told you a few home truths.' He smiled reminiscently. 'Then I knew that you were really a wild cat like your brothers. Not that I mind. I can handle wildcats.'

'I suppose you see yourself as Petruccio,' she said scathingly and assured herself that the reference would skim straight over his head.

'The Taming of the Shrew?' he asked lightly. 'Your father might care to cast me in the rôle but I'm not so anxious to have a Kate like you around my neck.'

'A very pretty compliment,' she said drily.

'I don't waste my time with compliments, as a rule. Certainly not on vain women. I prefer to tell the truth,' he said abruptly, rising to his feet. 'Come on. Let's eat.'

'You enjoy the masterful approach, don't you?' She made no move to leave her seat.

'Not particularly. It seems to come naturally – when you're around,' he said, resuming his seat. 'Do you want another drink?'

She nodded. 'Yes, I do.'

He took her glass with a faintly disapproving glance. 'You drink too much. It must be a common failing in your family.'

'If you're referring to Brent, he knows how to hold his drink,' she said hotly. 'No one else drinks too much in my family.'

'Surely one in a family is enough,' he commented as he nodded to the barman to refill the glasses.

'You really are quite different to anyone I've ever known,' she said demurely, toying with the refilled glass when it was placed in front of her.

He looked at her, suspicious of the sudden change of tone. 'Is that a good thing or not?'

'No one else has ever had the effrontery to run down my family to my face,' she told him sharply. Then with an abrupt movement she threw the contents of her glass into his face. 'I don't like it,' she told him viciously. She heard a shocked gasp from her neighbour but she did not care. It was the first time she had ever behaved quite so outrageously in a public place but she did not regret the insolent action.

Without a word he took his handkerchief from his pocket, mopped his face and then picked up his own glass. Suddenly wary, she moved apprehensively. He glanced coldly at her and tossed off the drink. Then he turned to the barman. 'Fill it up again,' he said and he sounded perfectly composed. Promise was a little disappointed that he had failed to retaliate, either with words or action, and she moved her shoulders in a tiny shrug of contempt for his lack of spirit. He raised the newly-filled glass and lifted it as though he were going to toast her. 'As I've said before, you're no lady,' he said quietly and deftly returned the compliment.

Promise gasped as the liqueur ran down her cheeks and stung her eyes. She was shocked beyond measure, incredulous that he could have done such a thing and dared to humiliate her so unbearably. He handed her his stained handkerchief courteously and she dabbed at her face, furious, humiliated and very near to tears of anger. 'Now that you know my tactics, you won't do that again in a hurry, will you?' he said smoothly. 'Go and fix your face and then we'll have lunch.'

His calm acceptance that she would be willing to remain with him astonished her.

Without a word she hurried from the bar and stared at the ravages of her make-up in the gleaming wall mirrors, horrified. The attendant stared at her curiously and Promise threw her a haughty glance. Suddenly she began to laugh. She might have expected it of Matt Nellin – he was ruthless and determined that she should not get the better of him and he would see no reason why he should not humiliate her equally as she had humiliated him. She knew a swift shaft of admiration. Her father would have been immensely amused and completely on Matt's side if he had been present. Her own behaviour left much to be desired and she could scarcely blame Matt for being so angry that he had sought to retaliate.

Hastily, she washed and applied fresh cosmetics to her lovely face. When she returned, Matt was sitting where she had left him, thoughtfully staring at the array of bottles behind the bar. She touched his shoulder. 'Let's have lunch,' she said lightly, ignoring the amused and speculative glances of the others in the bar.

He glanced at her and rose slowly to his feet. 'I didn't expect you to come back.'

She laughed up at him. 'That's exactly

why I did so, Matt.'

They went into the restaurant and while they waited for attention, he suddenly covered her hand with his own as she smiled at him. 'I'm sorry, Promise. That was quite unforgivable of me.'

'Forget it,' she told him smoothly. 'You're right, of course. I'll never throw a cocktail in your face again!'

He grinned reluctantly. 'We caused a sensation back there. This place isn't used to unruly clientele.'

'That was nothing,' she told him scornfully. 'Adam and Brent went to town in that bar one day and it cost my father five hundred pounds to repair the damage and keep their names out of the courts.' She chuckled. 'In five minutes they almost wrecked the place.'

'Let's agree not to discuss your brothers,' he said slowly. 'It only leads to arguments.' He studied her for a long moment and then immediately defied his own suggestion. 'Anyway, I think your pride in their stupid exploits is a little misjudged. That's something I could never understand in your old man. No matter what you do, what trouble you cause between you, he relates every incident with real pride and amusement.

Once he said something about it being the blood of the Irish. I suppose that's all it can be.'

Promise was surprised. 'Irish? There's nothing Irish about our blood, Matt.'

He raised an eyebrow. 'With that hair! If you ask me there's a great deal of Irish blood in all of you – and from what your father told me it comes from *his* father.'

Suddenly she remembered his claim that her grandfather had been a labourer and her grandmother a kitchen maid and hot, shamed colour stained her cheeks. She had been determined to question her father but in her anxiety for Russ it had slipped her mind.

She changed the subject decisively and after a moment he followed the lead. The meal was excellent and Promise proved that she had a healthy appetite. Matt ate with relish, also, and they conversed amiably during the meal.

She had recovered from the incident in the bar but she still felt the unreasonable dislike for Matt Nellin. Or was it so unreasonable, she asked herself shrewdly. He had proved himself ill-mannered, uncouth and un-gracious. She disliked his casual ways, the mockery which lingered so frequently in his eyes and in his smile, the undisguised contempt he felt for her – and because she had never been treated with anything but courtesy and admiration and deference it was quite a blow to her pride and angered her continually.

Despite all that her father had done for him, he could still condemn him and his family without hesitation. Despite the fact that he and Promise were complete strangers to each other, he had attempted to make love to her on the night of their first meeting. This she did not object to so much, regarding it as proof of the effect of her looks and personality. But she strongly resented his audacity in stripping away the veneer of her shy modesty and sweetness to reveal the true woman beneath without any consideration for her feelings. She had been angry and humiliated and she had never forgiven him for daring to know more of her than she revealed to anyone outside her family.

He had been solely to blame for Russ's daredevil pranks with Tempest – and because of Matt, Russ lay in a hospital bed, his head healing slowly and his spine terribly injured with the almost certain knowledge that he would never again walk without difficulty or be able to mount a horse. He had encouraged Sally Whitlock to presume herself engaged to Russ – a fact that her brother vehemently denied in the same breath that he steadfastly refused to see Sally if she was allowed to visit him.

He had persuaded her father that Jonothan's wish to enter a monastery was both sincere and wise for a boy with a natural austerity of outlook and too much sensitivity for happiness in the outside world. Jonothan was now studying Theology at an ecclesiastical college in order to acquaint himself with the new religion which would become his entire life.

Also, Matt had dared to humiliate her only that day and she knew that word of the incident would soon be on everyone's lips among her friends and acquaintances. She felt her anger rising against him once more...

CHAPTER ELEVEN

Coffee before them and cigarettes alight, she eyed Matt Nellin with dislike. He looked up and caught her gaze. An eyebrow shot up rapidly. 'Why so frigid? Decided to detest me again just when we were getting on so well? We haven't exchanged a cross word in almost an hour.'

'I haven't changed my original opinion of you,' she informed him coldly.

'That suits me,' he retorted swiftly. 'I haven't much time for you either, Promise Power.' He was enraged by the deep loathing he had surprised in her eyes and told himself he was a fool to put himself out to be pleasant to her merely because he was fond of Stephen Power!

Her eyes blazed. 'Then we must both hope that this is our last meeting.'

'It will be if I have anything to do with it,' he told her firmly. 'The next time your old man tries to force your company on me I shall regretfully plead a previous engagement!'

'I'll make sure he doesn't do anything of the kind again!'

He grinned maliciously. 'I guess your father's romantic notions have been firmly nipped in the bud,' he said drily.

She looked at him swiftly. 'What romantic notions, Mr Nellin?'

'Didn't you know that he has it all cut and dried? He had plans for the marriage of his only daughter to a promising young designer in his employ,' he said caustically.

'I thought he was talking nonsense,' she said slowly, puzzled. Then she tossed her head. 'However, the idea certainly doesn't attract me, I can assure you. My father's plans are doomed to disappointment.'

'Don't worry your pretty head! They weren't my plans if that's what you thought! I'm not likely to let him force me into taking you on for the rest of my life, either. I can think of far more preferable fates,' he told her hotly.

'As long as we both understand the position,' she said haughtily. 'Believe me Mr Nellin, I wouldn't marry you even if my father…'

'Cut you out of his will?' he finished for her, breaking into her words. 'Well, that sounds pretty drastic. I guess I'm safe enough, then.' He curtly turned away to summon their waiter. As he threw enough money to cover the bill on to the tray, Promise gathered up her gloves and bag and rose to her feet.

'Thanks for the lunch – or should I save my thanks for my father as he's footing the bill?' she asked cuttingly as he followed her from the restaurant. Without waiting for a reply she continued: 'Don't forget to present him with a full account of your expenditure on me!'

'You needn't remind me,' he said harshly. 'I only pay for my *pleasures!*'

Reluctantly but aware that she had left her sports car outside her father's office, Promise stepped into the taxi which came at his bidding. He hesitated briefly, then he shrugged and followed her into the dark and gloomy interior of the cab. Not a word was exchanged between them and they ignored each other until they turned into the narrow, busy thoroughfare dominated by the gleaming white building of the Power Construction Company. Then Matt seized her roughly in his arms and kissed her, hard and fierce. She was too taken aback to protest or struggle and for days afterwards she was angry with herself because she returned his kiss in that moment, too startled not to respond to the eager seeking warmth of his mouth. The knowledge that his unexpected kiss had given her pleasure and a strange thrill only added fuel to her anger.

She wrenched away and the look of dire wrath and hatred in her eyes haunted him for many a day. As she stepped from the taxi, she turned on her heel and walked to her car without a backward glance. Matt shrugged his broad shoulders, paid off the taxi and walked from the warm sunshine into the equally bright interior of the building.

He refused to allow the thought of Promise to intrude into his work and he doggedly concentrated on the difficult but interesting blueprint before him.

He did not regret that parting kiss. He had been determined to know the rough sweetness of her lips and the soft proximity of her lovely body just once – and he had risked a repeat of her previous spiteful behaviour. To his surprise her lips had parted eagerly beneath his own – and for the briefest of moments he had known ardent response before she stiffened and tore herself from his arms. He thought he would never forget the look in her eyes until his dying day. Anger and outrage and, what was incredibly hurtful, revulsion blazed at him from those wide grey eyes. So his kiss had repelled her! Well, he didn't give a damn. Perhaps for the first time in her life she had really known what it meant to be kissed by a man who knew his subject!

Stephen Power stumped from the lift and entered his office, grinning broadly. 'So you're back – earlier than I expected. Didn't Promise come back with you?'

'Only as far as the door,' he returned grimly.

Stephen perched his heavy body on the edge of the desk and studied him with amusement. 'Was it heavy going, my boy?'

'You knew it would be, didn't you?' Matt demanded roughly, suddenly aware of the older man's motive in asking him to take Promise to lunch.

Stephen nodded and chuckled richly. 'The girl has done nothing but tell me how much she dislikes you for some time. I thought it was about time she found out that you're quite a likeable chap.'

'Well, I'm sorry to disappoint you but I very much doubt if your daughter will welcome any attempts on your part to throw us together. We parted on extremely bad terms,' he said grimly.

'As bad as that, eh?' Stephen asked with interest. 'I'm glad to hear it.'

Matt threw him a suspicious glance. 'I'd like to know what little game you're playing, Steve!'

'I daresay you would,' he retorted smoothly. 'But surely an old man is allowed to amuse himself with a quiet game of chess.'

'Not when innocent people are your pawns,' Matt said quietly.

Stephen laughed. 'Promise isn't innocent – so don't you think it, my boy.'

'She is where your intentions are concerned – and so am I! Anyway, whatever the game, it isn't going to work out, Steve. Promise and I cordially detest each other!'

'Well, well. Who would have believed it?' Stephen said with malicious humour. As abruptly as he entered he strode towards the door. 'You're busy, my boy. I won't disturb you any longer.' Chuckling, he left the room and returned to his own offices.

Miss Framley glanced at him curiously as he passed her desk, recognising his mood and wondering what had happened to put him into such good humour.

Stephen carefully chose a cigar and nipped the end with great precision. He took a long time lighting it for his thoughts were far from his liking for cigars.

He was extremely fond of Matt Nellin and, if it had been possible, he would have provided for him generously in his will where the Company was concerned. But he was not blind to his duty to his sons and he still clung to the hope that one of them might yet show an inclination to follow in his footsteps. But if Matt were to become his son-in-law...

Well, that would be a different matter entirely. He could safely leave his shares in the Company to Promise with the proviso that her husband was to become Managing Director. He knew that Matt was both able and responsible and he had more respect for his business acumen than for that of any of his sons.

At the moment, Matt and Promise might 'cordially detest each other', in the boy's own words but in his experience that was a promising state of affairs. Far better than an infatuation which sprung to life too swiftly and died with even more speed. Better by far than indifference which could not be overcome. Let them detest each other now:

he felt certain that within six months they would be unable to live without each other.

They were well suited. He felt sure of that. Promise needed a masterful man and Matt was well able to handle her – she might balk at first but eventually she would realise that his decisions were the wise, the sensible and the honest ones. Matt was every inch a man – his excellent physique and handsome features rivalled those of his sons but he could claim the additional assets of brain, common sense, integrity and several steady qualities so completely lacking in his sons.

He had brought about their initial meeting and he had been well-pleased with the result. He knew that Matt was shrewd enough to see through Promise's mild deception which had fooled so many people and he also knew that Matt was too con-temptuous of poseurs to fail to emphasise his contempt and give Promise every oppor-tunity to betray the wild rebellion which seethed beneath her demure appearance.

Contrary to his daughter, he did not blame Matt for the foolishness which had led to a sojourn in hospital, for Russ. He understood that Promise had goaded him to display his equestrian skill and it was only to be expected that Russ would immediately be fired with the wish to outdo the more experienced man. His fall had been unfortunate. He constantly grieved that Russ would never again be as strong and powerful, a man to admire whether or not his personality inspired liking. He had taken a great fancy to little Sally Whitlock and he firmly believed her story of Russ's frequent proposals and her own refusals until Matt had made her realise that Russ had needed her even before his accident and that she would be even more necessary to him in the future. He knew that Sally was hurt by Russ's adamant insistence that he did not wish to see her and that he had never had any intention of marrying her. Stephen did not believe his son. Knowing the pride of the Powers he swiftly understood that Russ would not allow a girl like Sally to tie herself to him in his present invalid state – and he was warmed by the realisation that this time Russ was really in love and thinking of someone else before himself.

He had been fully prepared for Matt's persuasive tongue where Jonothan was concerned and as he did not mind what the boy chose to do with his life as long as he was happy he soon agreed to Matt's suggestion of an ecclesiastical college for a couple of years, and, later on, a monastery of Jonothan's own choice. He was perceptive enough to see the wisdom of Matt's arguments. They had been quite unnecessary for he had never entertained any notion of interfering with Jonothan's decision. But it had been pleasant to pretend otherwise and give Matt the chance to wield his cleverly persuasive defence which he enjoyed hearing.

He had been vaguely disappointed when Matt showed no interest in seeing Promise again but had comforted himself with the thought that they were certain to meet again from time to time. She had played into his hands by coming to London on a day when it was impossible for her father to take her out to lunch. His first thought when Miss Framley notified him of his daughter's arrival was that here was an opportunity, too good to be missed, for Promise and Matt to learn a little more about each other. The very fact that each was so vehement in their protestations of dislike amused him and encouraged him to believe that their violence of emotion was born of something that went much deeper and was far more lasting than ordinary dislike...

Meanwhile, Promise battled with the

heavy traffic of the great metropolis, impatient to leave behind the busy roads and make her way home as quickly as possible. She tore furiously at the wheel of her expensive sports car and swerved violently to avoid an absent-minded pedestrian who stepped into her path. She let loose a flood of angry invective and the scared pedestrian stared after her in astonishment.

Halted by traffic lights, watching the indicators anxiously and impatiently, she did not notice the approach of a tall, attractive man whose blond hair gleamed in the sunshine. His fair, pleasant face belied his character and Promise was not the only one to be deceived by his looks and manner.

Easily, without pause, he opened the car door and slid into the seat beside Promise who turned swiftly, started and said lightly: 'Oh, it's you!'

'Yes, it's me,' Tyler Bradford agreed smoothly, smiling at her. 'Going my way?'

She laughed, amused by his suave presumption. 'It looks like it, doesn't it? Where are you going?'

'The lights have changed,' he told her and his words were confirmed by the impatient sounding of horns from the cars behind.

She let in the clutch and the car shot past the traffic lights. 'Why not park around the corner and have coffee with me?' Ty suggested.

Within a few moments she had found a parking space and neatly drew into it. Then she turned to smile at him. 'What are you doing in Town?'

He shrugged. 'Trying to amuse myself. But it's very flat just now. It was a relief to recognise your car, sweet Promise.'

'I've been buying a few things,' she told him and carelessly indicated a pile of parcels in the back of the car. 'I was just on my way home.' Her smile was sweet and faintly shy for it was almost second nature to switch on the generally accepted pose.

He grinned. 'Then you can give me a lift when we've had some coffee – if you will?'

'Oh, of course,' she agreed.

They walked along the pavements to a coffee house and were soon seated in a quiet corner of the little restaurant with its futuristic décor. While Ty brought out cigarettes and a lighter, she glanced at him covertly through her long lashes, a faint glint of humour in her eyes. She had known him for several years for he was one of Brent's closest friends. While still in her teens, Promise had known a violent infatuation for the good-looking, debonair man with the smooth manner and his indulgence for light flirtation. A few years older with a preference for more sophisticated companions, he had scarcely looked in her direction, accepting her without question or thought as Brent's sister. Eventually she had forgotten her girlish dreams of him in the thrill and triumph of her various conquests. But even to this day she knew a familiar pounding of her heart and a tremor of excitement whenever he spoke to her directly or invited her to dance with him or smiled at her across a crowded room.

Ty was fully aware of that and it amused him to seek her out occasionally without serious intention. He was sometimes puzzled by her apparent sweetness and demure modesty, comparing her lack of wildness and unsullied reputation with that of her brothers. If any of her many love affairs had been fast and furious then he had never heard about it – and he cynically assumed that the reason why she was still unmarried and had no constant escort was because she preferred to keep her good name than to move with the times. A promiscuous man himself, he could understand the reluctance of his fellow men to tie themselves to a woman completely lacking in passion.

He looked up and there was something in her gaze that caught his attention. For the first time, he wondered if there was more to Promise Power than met the eye at first glance. Always willing for a new adventure, he decided to follow up that hint of an invitation in her eyes. So he smiled at her warmly and offered his cigarettes, looking long and intimately into her eyes as she leaned forward to accept a light. Failing to meet the rebuff he expected his pulses began to race slightly and he knew the sweet exhilaration which always attacked him at the thought of a new conquest.

Cleverly, to lull any suspicions that she might have, he drew her into casual conversation and within a few minutes they were discussing Brent's unexpected engagement and Russ's accident with the ease of long association.

Sensing his interest, Promise played up to him, both pleased and flattered that at long last she was beginning to excite his admiration – and determined, though she would not admit this, to erase the memory of Matt Nellin in the arms of another man – particularly a man like Tyler Bradford who had always been a subject for speculation on her part. If she had suspected his ruthless intentions she might have hesitated but she was quite willing to undertake a mild affair with him and she encouraged him eagerly but careful not to betray the real woman behind her pose of shy, modest and sweet Promise Power.

By the time they reached his home, a few miles from her own, they were on warm, almost intimate terms and he pressed her fingers fervently before he swung out of the car and waited to wave her on her way.

As she entered the house, the telephone shrilled and she walked across to it. Giving the number, she heard Ty's voice in response.

'I say, Promise – I don't know why I didn't think to ask you before. I'm going to a party tonight. Quite a small affair. Would you care to come with me?'

'I don't want to gatecrash,' she said, with pretty hesitation.

'I was told to take a friend with me,' he assured her. 'I meant to go alone, as a matter of fact, but now I think it would be more enjoyable in your company,' he added, mentally making a note to telephone his current girl-friend and change their plans for the evening.

'I should like that,' she said eagerly. 'Where is the party? Do I know your host?'

'You should do,' he returned and his smile touched his voice with warmth. 'Willis Freeman is having a quiet celebration on behalf of his recent success in his college exams.'

'He passed his finals? Oh, I am pleased,' she exclaimed. 'Why, I'd love to go, Ty. How nice of you to ask me!'

'The pleasure will be mine, sweet,' he said easily. 'I'll call for you at eight.'

Replacing the receiver, Promise executed a few, light-hearted dance steps across the massive hall. Adam stood in the doorway of the library, watching her without expression. As she caught sight of him, she came to a standstill. 'Oh, hallo, Adam.'

'Did you have lunch with Father?' he asked, without great interest.

She pursed her lips impatiently. 'No, he had an appointment. I lunched with that beastly Matt Nellin.'

He raised an eyebrow. 'If you dislike him so much, why lunch with him?' he asked reasonably.

'Oh, Father pushed him on to me and I

194

couldn't get out of it,' she returned easily. She walked by him into the library and Julie Wentworth smiled at her from the depths of a comfortable armchair. 'Oh Julie! I didn't know you were here,' she said, a little surprised.

'Adam tells me you've been to Town. I hope your father was in a good mood,' Julie said in her brittle, sophisticated voice.

'Why?' Promise asked bluntly.

Adam walked over to Julie and put his hand on her shoulder. 'Because Julie and I were married this morning – and I don't think he's going to be very pleased about it.'

'Married. Heavens, no, Adam, he isn't! You know he's been set against the idea from the beginning,' she exclaimed.

Adam and Julie exchanged glances. Then Julie laughed. 'Well, he can't do anything about it now, can he? We're married and we're both of age to do as we please.'

'Do your parents know?'

She shook her head. 'No one knows except you, Promise.'

Promise threw her brother a reproachful glance. 'Well, I don't see why it had to be so sudden – and so underhand,' she said coolly. She had never cared much for Julie Wentworth and now, gazing at her smug,

195

triumphant expression, she disliked her even more.

'The good old *fait accompli*,' Julie said lightly. 'My father thinks Adam is too irresponsible and reckless to make a good husband. Your father doesn't like me and never wanted Adam to think of marrying me. Rather than put up with a great many arguments we decided to marry first and argue second.'

'Well, if you love each other...' Promise trailed off with a shrug.

'Don't be so naïve,' Adam said impatiently. 'You know very well that if I'm to get that money of Grandfather's I must be married before I'm thirty. Well, I'm thirty next month – and Julie's as good as anyone when it comes to taking a wife.'

Promise stared at him. She had completely forgotten the condition of her grandfather's will and she felt sure that only Adam would be likely to have remembered it. She turned to Julie. 'What about you? Were you prepared to marry Adam for the sake of that money?'

'It's scarcely your concern,' Julie replied with a trace of indignation. 'But if you must know I married Adam because I'm tired of living at home and being petted because I'm the only child. I don't mind being spoiled but I do object to having my parents watch my every move. I can't take even the slightest interest in a man without having to answer a hundred questions about him and my intentions and feelings and listening to warnings galore!'

Dryly, Promise said: 'It doesn't seem to have spoiled your fun, Julie.'

Hostility flashed between the two women and Adam hastily stepped in. 'So I get my money and Julie gets more freedom than she's had in the past. A satisfactory arrangement where we're concerned even if no one else likes it.'

'Where will you live?' Promise wanted to know.

'Adam thought we could take a flat in Town,' Julie replied. 'I'm bored to death with the country and there's always plenty of social life in Town.'

'You mean plenty of men to amuse you,' Promise snapped.

'Possibly. But Adam won't be a Victorian husband, will you, darling? And there'll be no leading strings for him, either. Oh, we shall rub along well enough, I expect.'

'It might suit you but I'm damned if I'd marry any man for such ridiculous reasons,'

Promise said vehemently.

'Remember your Mrs Beeton,' Julie retorted sweetly and Promise flushed with anger. 'First find a man willing to marry you! How old are you now, dear? Twenty-three? But perhaps you're not in any hurry to settle down with one man and, according to rumour, no man is in a hurry to settle down with you!'

Promise threw her a scornful glance, her eyes flashing dangerously, then she stalked from the room without a word.

In the seclusion of her own room, thrusting Estelle out with an injunction to bring in her parcels from the car, she sat down on her bed and thought of her father's reaction to Adam's marriage. Julie's words, taunting and feline, rang in her ears. She was twenty-three, it was true, and no man had ever proposed marriage to her, although she had known her fair share of men-friends. Was it possible that Julie's approach resulted in speedier success than her own? She could not believe that Adam and Julie would have married without any affection for each other, no matter how lightly they might shrug aside the suggestion. But she didn't want to get married! She was enjoying life well enough and when she did decide to marry there would be men enough to choose from! Surely no man could believe that she was really sweet and shy – and dull in comparison with Julie? Surely any man with intelligence could sense the exciting, intoxicating warmth and passion behind the adopted façade? But that implied that she would have to attribute intelligence to Matt Nellin whose swift perception had been both insulting and unwelcome!

CHAPTER TWELVE

The nine days' wonder of Adam's un-expected marriage soon blew over and was forgotten. He found a flat in Town and they moved into it within a month, spending the preliminary weeks with her parents who were speedily reconciled to their daughter's action when she reminded them of Stephen Power's wealth and the almost-certainty that Adam would inherit the lion's share.

Russ left hospital for his home, his frac-tured skull having healed satisfactorily and swiftly, and two large, pleasant rooms on the ground floor were converted into a bed-room and sitting-room for him. He soon became adept at handling his wheelchair and he was frequently to be found trundling from one room to another, his useless legs covered by a rug. Bitterness and the mem-ory of pain lurked in his grey eyes but his brilliant, cheerful smile was ever-present and Stephen Power discovered that he had an intelligent and amusing companion in the son whose active life had so tragically and abruptly been cut short.

Jonothan's letters were serene and happy and no one could doubt that for the first time in his life he had found a worthwhile direction for his thoughts and emotions.

Brent was spending most of his time with Nancy and seemed to be quite resigned to his future marriage, the plans already well in hand for the wedding.

Promise was seeing a great deal of Tyler Bradford, much to everyone's surprise. She enjoyed his company, his conversation which was full of amusing anecdotes and shrewd perception and the triumph of response to her renewed infatuation for him.

Stephen enjoyed talking of his family and he found an ever-ready ear in Matt Nellin. So it was that Matt knew of the activities and behaviour of the Power tribe, as he thought of them to himself. Matt was in full agreement when Stephen announced that he had washed his hands of Adam who could do such a foolhardy thing as to marry a girl like Julie Wentworth whose reputation was known all over the county and who could be relied upon to play him false time and again. He listened with sympathy to the recital of Russ's cheerfulness and amazing indifference to his wheelchair and assured Stephen that there was still reason to hope that Russ would begin to take an interest in the Company. As Stephen pointed out, there was nothing to stop the boy from being very useful even if he was a cripple and it would be a good thing if he could be persuaded to handle the accounts of the Company for mathematics had always been his strong point and once Stephen had hoped to make a financier out of his son.

Matt expressed pleasure that Jonothan was doing so well and confirmed Stephen's own opinion that the boy had always been cut out for a different life to the one he had known for twenty years. Stephen exclaimed that Jonothan had always had leanings towards religion and attributed it carelessly to the Catholic upbringing and faith of his own father, conveniently forgetting to add that the first Russell Power had been a drunkard who never set foot inside a church once he reached his teens and that his faith had been sorely neglected until shortly before he died when he demanded a priest and wallowed freely in remorse for his sins.

He substantiated Stephen's own approval of Brent's approaching wedding and listened politely while Stephen spoke at great length of Nancy and the possibility that Brent would settle down and realise his good fortune in having such a wife who was obviously very much in love with him and fully prepared to overlook his many faults.

But when Stephen began to speak of Promise, Matt suddenly found that there was a pile of work waiting for him or remembered a telephone call which must be made immediately or excused himself adroitly on an assumed pretext. He was not interested in the girl's new affair, had never met Tyler Bradford and privately thought that any man was fortunate if he escaped the wiles of Promise Power. He was indifferent to Stephen's suppositions as to her subsequent marriage to Tyler Bradford. He did not care whom she married or if she married at all. All he wanted was to be spared any reference to her or her father's indulgent singing of her praises. As far as he was concerned, Promise had no good qualities to laud and her father was blinded by his devotion. He devoutly hoped that there would be no further occasion to spend even five minutes in her company and if Stephen mentioned casually that Promise would be in Town and was likely to call at the office he immediately made arrangements to be elsewhere – preferably twenty miles away so that there was no chance of meeting her accidentally.

His strange reaction to her name was illogical and confusing. He did all in his power to avoid meeting or speaking of her – yet the mere sound of her name on Stephen Power's lips was sufficient impetus for the unexpected leap of his heart, the dryness of his lips and a swift rush of heat through his veins. Try as he might, he could not erase the memory of her lips beneath his own in swift, ardent response – and neither could he forget the equally swift revulsion in her eyes which contrasted so forcibly to that response.

At night, trying to sleep against the roar of late-night traffic which passed the huge block where he rented a small, masculine apartment, her face would suddenly appear before his eyes – beautiful, wilful and angry but with so much appeal to his senses that he moved restlessly, impatient with his disloyal thoughts and angry with his treacherous body which could desire with such aching intensity the woman he most detested.

At his desk, working feverishly on a set of plans or checking over blueprints, his thoughts would be invaded by a mocking reminder that as a man she would have none of him. He would conjure up an imaginary picture of Tyler Bradford, endowing him with all the most despicable faults he particularly disliked – and imagine Promise in his arms, giving her kisses willingly, laughing into his eyes and sweet-talking him, more content in his company than she had ever been in his own. Then he would shrug, tear up the sheet of rough paper on which he had been doodling her name idly and endlessly, and mentally congratulate himself on not having fallen victim to her peculiar charm. He would assure himself that she was welcome to Tyler Bradford and that the man would swiftly repent of any alliance he might undertake with Promise.

In the company of his friends, he would suddenly lapse into silence and stare hungrily across a crowded restaurant or peer into the dimness of a theatre audi-torium, believing briefly that a real image of Promise had flitted across his vision. His friends ragged him mercilessly and then he would laugh, shrug off the ridiculous obsession with a girl not worth a passing thought, and enter into the spirit of the evening with such zest and forced gaiety and reckless sense of adventure that they were bewildered by the revelation of a side of his nature they had never met before.

Occasionally, his eyes did not deceive him – and it would be Promise, seated at a table with a fair-headed man or a group of noisy companions or perhaps sitting a few rows away from him in a theatre seat, engrossed in the action on stage and too indifferent to those who surrounded her to scan the auditorium for a familiar face. But she either did not see him or did not deign to acknowledge him and he would suffer the tortures of the damned while she flirted openly and outrageously with the man who escorted her, his pride and his determined lack of interest in her preventing him from claiming her attention even for the briefest of courtesies.

The few women who had once known his attentions found him cold and aloof of late, and teased him about his absorption in another woman, assuring him that he had all the symptoms of a man in love. But he stoutly refuted such accusations and if they recurred to his mind from time to time he firmly told himself that he was being nonsensical and that love was the last thing in connection with his feelings towards Promise Power. When he fell in love, if ever, it would be with a woman who was malleable, even tempered and genuinely sweet by nature – it was odd that whenever he met such a woman he found her remarkably dull and lacking in spirit. There was no doubt that Promise was stimulating and exciting even if she aroused his most primitive instincts and made him feel savagely inclined to make her bend to his will by brute force!

When Stephen extended an invitation to him to spend a week-end at his mansion in the country, Matt racked his brains rapidly for a reasonable excuse for refusal that his employer and friend would accept without question.

Stephen grinned cheerfully. 'You needn't worry about Promise,' he said carelessly. 'She's spending the week-end with the Bradfords.'

Matt knew a strange sensation of disappointment which he dismissed swiftly. 'Well, I'm not sure that I can make it...' he began.

Stephen interrupted him. 'Think it over and let me know by the end of the week. You can travel down with me on Friday evening and return in time for work on Monday morning, if that suits you.' He nodded to Matt in friendly fashion and then turned back to the papers on his desk. Matt left the office, thoughtful. He knew that Stephen fully expected him to accept the invitation and there was in fact no reason why he should not. He was annoyed that Stephen had immediately seized on the true reason for his hesitation. There were many times when he ardently wished that he and Promise had not got off to such a bad start, that they could have been friends instead of such violent enemies, and he invariably hastily added the mental supplement: 'For the old man's sake!' It would obviously give Stephen Power great pleasure to know that his daughter and his most trusted employee were on good terms and Matt often felt guilty that he could not oblige the man he liked and respected so much. If Promise had been anything but the rebellious, deceitful little tramp that she definitely happened to be! If he had been willing to let her deceive him as to her disposition and character as she apparently deceived others! But he would not be false to himself for any man and he despised Promise for pretending to be other than herself.

Friday evening came – and Matt joined

Stephen in the comfortable back seat of the new Daimler. The drive was uneventful and companionable for Stephen and Matt always found plenty to discuss – and for once Stephen Power did not bring his family into the conversation.

As they entered the house, Russ manoeuvred his way through the library door and greeted Matt with a hearty shout of welcome. The two men shook hands and grinned at each other – and Matt carefully refrained from assisting Russ in turning his wheelchair and making his way back into the pleasant, panelled room. Stephen immediately crossed to the decanters and poured drinks for all of them. Matt sat down facing Russ and the two young men talked easily together without reference to the wheelchair or the accident which had made it necessary. Matt could not help a feeling of miserable guilt as he studied the handsome and virile young man, confined indefinitely to a wheelchair but with none of his zest for life deployed by his invalid state. He was careful not to mention Sally Whitlock's name, well primed by Stephen that it was the only subject which Russ consistently refused to discuss and which could revive the ghost of bitterness in his grey eyes.

Brent joined them within a few minutes and stood in the doorway, taking stock of Matt. Then he advanced to shake hands cordially and discuss their chances of riding over the week-end which threatened the continuance of wet weather. Matt shot a glance at Russ, fully expecting that the mention of horses would be painful to him, but he was listening eagerly and broke in swiftly to suggest that Matt might care to ride Tempest now that he was more willing to accept a saddle on his back. He said this with a cheerful, mischievous smile which earned Matt's respect – and he told himself that Russ was far more likeable now and might yet prove to be a good friend in the future, as well as a business associate.

Another drink – and then Stephen suggested that Matt would like to change for dinner and assured him that he would easily find his way to the room he had occupied on the last occasion he stayed at the house.

Matt was willing enough to fall in with the suggestion and he excused himself courteously. As he mounted the wide staircase, he heard a woman's voice raised in anger and he stiffened. Surely that sounded like Promise yet her father had assured him that she would be away for the week-end. He walked on, his heart pounding.

Then, just before he reached the open door of her bedroom, a brush hurtled into the passage – and a smile touched his lips. Promise was evidently in one of her wild tantrums.

'I've told you a hundred times to be careful with that zip!' Promise shouted angrily. 'Now what in merry hell am I to wear tonight, you stupid idiot? Oh, you're useless. I don't know why I didn't send you packing years ago … oh!' This last exclamation as she caught sight of Matt at the door with the brush in his hand and the trace of amusement in his eyes. 'What are *you* doing here?' she demanded rudely, confronting him with blazing eyes. An enchanting, ballerina-length dance dress of ice-blue tulle fell about her slim body and the bodice hung about her waist, useless because of the broken zip which fastened it from waist to nape of the neck. Her youthful, provocatively thrusting breasts were concealed by the merest wisp of flimsy underwear and her white shoulders, the creamy curve of throat and breasts, back, arms and midriff were completely bare. With her beautiful, rich auburn hair falling past her shoulders in silken, glossy masses, her wide grey eyes flashing angrily and her tiptilted nose a mass of freckles, she was an attractive picture – and Matt drew in his breath sharply.

She suddenly realised the extent of her dishabillé and she snatched up a silk robe and pulled it about her. 'Don't you know better than to march into a woman's bedroom?'

He handed the brush to the nervous Estelle who hovered between him and Promise. 'You shouldn't leave your door wide open when you're dressing,' he remarked mildly.

'Get out!'

He did not move. 'Maybe I can fix that zip. I'm quite handy at that kind of thing.' He smiled but there was no real warmth in his expression. 'It seems a pity that your evening will be ruined because of a broken zip.'

'The dress is unimportant,' she told him coldly. 'Do you think I've nothing else in my wardrobe? Please get out and close the door behind you!'

'Say, you're learning some manners at last. Must you spoil my impression of you?'

Without replying she moved swiftly,

pushed him into the wide corridor and slammed the door on him. With a chuckle, he walked on to his own room, ignoring the faint perturbation he felt because she was, after all, at the house.

While he bathed and changed into formal suit, he tried in vain to forget the enchanting picture of Promise with her hair falling about her slim, lovely body which had provocatively invited his admiration and aroused swift desire. Setting his lips and adjuring himself not to be dazzled by her undeniable beauty, he went down to join his host in a drink before dinner.

To his disappointment, Promise did not join them for the meal. She came into the drawing-room in a cloud of primrose chiffon, her hair banded about her proud head in a copy of an old-fashioned Victorian style which gave her demurity and striking beauty. Accepting a drink from her father, she went directly to the attack.

'You didn't tell me that Mr Nellin was to be here for dinner, Father. I would have changed my plans for the evening.' This with a malicious glance at Matt which informed him that she would have done nothing of the kind.

Stephen smiled and slipped his arm about

her bare shoulders. 'Didn't I, my darling? It must have slipped my mind. But Matt's here for the week-end – and you're spending a few days with the Bradfords, aren't you? Badly arranged on my part, eh?'

She tilted her chin. 'Not at all. I'm sure that Mr Nellin will be amply entertained without my efforts.'

Brent broke in. 'Sure! Riding and shooting and perhaps a little fishing – men's amusements, eh, Matt? A woman would only be in the way.'

Promise was immediately indignant. 'I can ride and shoot as well as any of you, Brent. And I've never been accused of disturbing you while you fish. Be fair at all costs!'

Brent grinned. 'Watch that temper! One of these days it will get you into trouble.'

She turned her back on her brother. 'Ty is calling for me,' she told her father. 'I expect he'll be here in a minute.'

'Where are you going tonight?' he asked indulgently. 'Dancing in that dress, I'll be bound.'

She shrugged. 'That new roadhouse on the By-Pass, I expect. Ty is anxious to sample its amusements.' The sound of an impatient horn caused her to finish her drink hastily and thrust the glass into Matt's hand. 'Take this, will you? Ty hates to be kept waiting.' She flashed him a cool, contemptuous smile. 'Enjoy your week-end, Mr Nellin.'

'Thanks.' He spoke curtly, pained by her eagerness to appease Tyler Bradford's impatience, which seemed so out of character for Promise. He did not doubt for a moment that her readiness to run at his bidding had its roots in her reluctance to stay in the same room with him for any length of time.

The dinner to which they presently adjourned was excellently cooked and served but Matt scarcely touched the food set before him. He toyed with his wine-glass and tried to dismiss the sense of unease which attacked him. He wondered if Promise was enjoying her evening. He wondered what type of man was Tyler Bradford and if Promise really was so smitten by his charms as her father feared. Thinking of her radiant beauty that evening and aware of the assault on his own senses he wondered if Tyler Bradford had enough self-control to keep his hands off Promise that night. But then he chided himself mockingly. If he did, Promise would be exceedingly disappointed. Men and their attentions were the spice of life to her. For all he knew, she was Tyler's mistress and had been for several weeks – and the anguish which swept over him at the thought was almost unbearable.

The conversation flowed over his head for the main part but he managed to keep up his part in it with courteous if noncommital remarks. The week-end's entertainments, outlined by Brent, seemed to have lost their flavour since it was obvious that Promise was to have no part of them. He had been adamant in his decision to refuse Stephen Power's suggestion if Promise was to be at the house but now, finding that she had removed her presence without hesitation, he thought illogically that the days stretched before him long and interminably and would no doubt be extremely dull without Promise to liven them for him. Mocking himself for his weakness where she was concerned, he told himself that he would enjoy the week-end much more without the constant wrangles and icy hostility which killed any pretence of sufferance on either side.

CHAPTER THIRTEEN

The meal over, Brent suggested that he might like to walk across the fields to a quiet and friendly pub where they could have a drink and some masculine conversation. Matt noticed that Russ glanced suspiciously at his brother but made no comment. Stephen urged Matt to do exactly as he pleased and assured him that he need feel no compulsion to spend his time with his host.

So the two men strode across the fields, over the tiny stone bridge and through the dark, sombre copse – which, Brent assured him, was lovely enough while the sun streamed through the foliage and turned each clearance into a colourful and peaceful glade – and along the country lanes to the pub which turned out to be the *Crooked Scythe*. Matt had vaguely expected this and he turned an enquiring glance on Brent.

'Isn't this where Sally Whitlock lives?'

Brent nodded. 'I walk down here occasionally to let her know how Russ is getting on and to cheer her up. She's pretty miserable these days. He still won't have anything to do with her, the damn fool! She's a nice kid and she'd do anything for Russ – even marry him tomorrow, helpless as he is. But no one can get near the subject with him,' he finished angrily.

'Sally still remains faithful, does she?' Matt asked and realised his mistake as Brent turned on him wrathfully.

'What do you think? That I'm sneaking behind my own brother's back to make love to his girl? Because she's still his girl in everyone's eyes but his, believe me!'

'Don't pick me up so quickly,' Matt said, laughing, and knocking aside Brent's balled fists. 'You're more than a match for me, Brent. I didn't mean anything of the kind. I was merely surprised that she still hopes to marry him even though she knows how he feels on the subject.' He looked at Brent with new eyes, more surprised that the man should be so concerned with the unhappiness of Sally Whitlock when everyone had it that none of the Powers were concerned with anyone but themselves.

'Nothing will persuade her that it's hopeless,' Brent returned as they pushed open the door to the saloon and ducked their heads to avoid the low beam of the ceiling. They went down three shallow steps and found the ceiling to be high enough for them to straighten up. Sally was behind the bar, talking cheerfully to three of the local men, but she glanced up with a bright smile for Brent – and then a swift, surprised smile for Matt. As soon as she could, she walked to their end of the bar.

'Hallo, Brent – the usual? Good evening, Mr Nellin.'

'Matt,' he amended with a warm smile for her. 'Nice to meet you again, Sally. I thought you'd be married to Russ by now.'

Her face clouded but she turned to fill a glass with whiskey for Brent which she placed before him. 'Are you having whiskey too?' she asked Matt.

'No, I'll try some of your old-fashioned country beer. Brent has been singing its praises all the way here – and now the traitor drinks whiskey!'

Sally smiled and pulled a foaming glass of ale for him. She shook her head when Matt offered payment. 'The first is always on the house for Brent. My father's orders.'

Matt raised an eyebrow. 'I had the feeling that Brent wasn't very popular down here. Or is this one pub where the Power boys don't stir up trouble?' he asked, ribbing Brent who grinned.

'Oh, they're much milder these days,' Sally said quickly. 'But my Dad used to say that people came halfway across the county in the hope of watching the Powers mix it with the locals. He didn't mind a few breakages as long as he had the extra custom.'

Matt laughed. 'Well, that's a new slant. As a rule, publicans steer well clear of trouble.'

They chafed each other lightly for a few minutes then Matt said quietly as Brent turned away to engage one of the local men in conversation: 'It must be some time since you've seen Russ.'

'Yes, it is,' she returned and seemed reluctant to continue the conversation.

As she moved away on the pretence of wiping the polished bartop, he caught her wrist and smiled at her warmly. 'Why don't you just take the bull by the horns?'

She looked puzzled. 'What do you mean?'

'Russ refuses to have you visit him – won't even have your name mentioned. It seems to me that he's still in love with you, nevertheless. Perhaps longing to see you. Why don't you walk back with Brent and me and just go in to Russ? He can't very well turn you out of the house – and it's my guess that he'll be so pleased to see you that he won't even wonder how you managed to get in!'

'I couldn't do that!' she gasped.

'Of course you could. Nothing easier! I think it's the only thing to do.'

She shook her head doubtfully. 'It would only make matters worse.' She sighed briefly. 'I must just be patient and wait till Russ asks to see me. I *know* he will eventually.'

'You might wait a long time,' he told her. Then he shrugged. 'But if you don't mind throwing your life away...'

He dropped the subject and turned to talk to Brent as his companion finished his conversation. But he watched Sally closely and he noticed the changes in her expression as she continued to serve and wash glasses. She was still bright and cheerful but he firmly believed that now it did not come so easily. He had given her food for thought.

Some time later, just as Brent glanced at his watch and murmured that it was about time they walked back, she came up to them. 'I think you're right, Matt,' she said breathlessly, evidently having forced herself to find the necessary courage. 'If Brent doesn't mind, I will come with you.'

Brent looked startled. 'What's that?' Matt hastily explained and he looked dubious for a moment, then he grinned. 'Good idea. The best thing to do, as Matt says, Sally. Russ can't object until it's too late – and at least you'll have seen him for a few minutes even if he refuses to talk to you!'

Retracing their steps in the darkness which had fallen, Matt was very conscious of Sally's hand on his arm and of the nervousness which filled her small body. Now and again he pressed her fingers reassuringly. It seemed a much longer walk back to the house than it had been to the *Crooked Scythe* and as they gradually neared their destination, Matt found himself wondering if he had been wise to put the idea into Sally's head. It was quite possible that everyone was deceived about Russ's feelings. It could well be that he had long forgotten his love for Sally and really had no wish to see her or talk about her. Sally – Brent and Matt too, being in the conspiracy – would look a fine fool and undergo a humiliating experience if Russ bluntly pointed out his lack of interest in her.

A light shone from the library window as they mounted the stone steps to the terrace. Brent glanced at Matt. 'That's where he'll be. He usually sits in the library in the evening. I never knew he had such a liking for books until he was forced to give up his horses and social life.'

They paused outside the windows of the library and Sally began to tremble slightly. Brent gave her a little push. 'Go on in. Faint heart never won fair Russ,' he misquoted cheerfully. 'At least he can't eat you, Sally.'

Her hand on the pane, she hesitated and glanced from one to the other of the two men. Brent nodded reassuringly and Matt smiled at her with a hint of real affection.

Suddenly resolute, she pushed open the window and stepped into the room. Brent took Matt's arm and they went further along the terrace and entered the house by the windows of the drawing-room.

Russ was reading, his head bowed over a book. Sally stood watching him for some minutes and he was quite unaware of her presence in the room. Occasionally he picked up a pencil and a notebook and hastily scrawled some notation. He was completely engrossed. The soft lighting fell on his auburn hair which gleamed bronzely and his profile was illumined to tenderness. Studying him, Sally thought how much he had changed. He no longer seemed like the rip-roaring, reckless and rebellious Russ Power whom she had loved since she was barely a child. But her love for him was not diminished because of the sudden enforced peace and submission which had changed him so much. Her love swelled to infinite measures – and she took a step towards him, her eyes bright with her love and her lips parted with eagerness.

He swung his wheelchair round abruptly – and stared at her for a long moment in complete disbelief and amazement. Not a word was spoken by either of them. Words did not seem necessary in that moment. Then he held out his hand to her and his grey eyes welcomed her with a swift flaring of the love which had never left him during the long weeks of exile from this innocent country girl with her own simple claims to beauty.

She ran to him and knelt before him, cradled in his arms, his cheek pressed against her hair – and it was a long time before anything was said. Then they spoke so incoherently of their love for each other and the only possible outcome of that love that it would have been difficult for an outsider to follow their declarations and promises and husky, ardent compensations for the weeks of separation.

Brent and Matt waited anxiously. They had told Sally to come to the drawing-room if Russ refused to speak to her or turned her from the library. Minutes passed and there was no sign of the girl.

At last, Brent turned to Matt with a grin. 'I guess that's done the trick. Now perhaps there'll be no more nonsense and I can spend my evenings with Nancy rather than drinking whiskey and beer I don't want at the *Crooked Scythe!*'

Matt raised an eyebrow. 'Don't tell me you've a yen to become teetotal because I won't believe it!'

Brent laughed. 'Nancy's father keeps a supply of very creditable whiskey – and Nancy ensures that I don't drink too much of it.'

'How long is it now till your wedding?'

'Three weeks,' Brent returned. 'If I had to wait much longer I'd bust. Nancy went all virtuous on me as soon as we were engaged!' he added ruefully and Matt could not help but laugh at the expression in the man's eyes.

'I get the impression that you don't feel too badly about assuming the responsibilities of a married man,' Matt said with a mocking gleam in his eyes.

'It'll probably be hell for both of us – but if I must marry – and everyone seems to think it's a man's only fate! – then I'd rather marry Nancy than anyone else. She may look as dull as ditchwater but I warn you not to upset her!' He touched the faint scar on his cheek. 'I'm more careful these days. I don't intend to give her another excuse for taking a riding crop to me!' After a pause, he went on: 'Beats me why my father is anxious to marry us off. I should have thought the Powers had caused enough trouble in this part of the world without having a few more around to make life more precarious.'

Stephen heard his son's words as he came into the room. 'The Powers may be un-popular but we have the entrée to every respectable house in the country,' he retorted sharply. 'Money buys anything, my son – but sometimes I like to think our respectable neighbours enjoy a little excite-ment occasionally. And there's nothing like a Power to ensure that!' He handed round cigars, a sure sign that he was in a genial mood. 'I must go and shake Russ out of his books or the boy will get too dull. All work and no light relief won't do him any good.' He strode to the door to be checked by a unanimous exclamation from Brent and Matt. He looked from one to the other in surprise. 'What the devil are you boys cooking up now?' he demanded.

Before he could reply, Brent swung to the door, his keen ears having caught the sound of rubber wheels on the parquet flooring of the hall. He threw it open and Russ, eyes shining with a new radiance, his whole bearing altered abruptly, manoeuvred his way into the room with Sally close behind him.

'There's your answer,' Brent said with a grin.

Stephen beamed on his son and the young girl. 'So you've finally got together?'

'Only because Brent and Matt persuaded me to take the...' Sally broke off in confusion, swift colour flooding her piquant face in embarrassment.

Russ laughed. 'Take the bull by the horns, eh? Well, it was sound advice. I might have wallowed in my pride so long that you didn't want to marry me any more, Sally.' He caught her hand and pressed it to his lips, oblivious of the presence of the others.

'Another wedding?' Stephen gave a mock sigh. 'This house will be echoing with emptiness, soon,' he told them with assumed dismay.

'No, it won't!' Russ retorted. 'Sally and I are going to live here just to plague you for a few more years – and with any luck there'll be the patter of tiny feet to wake you in the early hours before any of us are much older!'

'Don't count your chickens before they're hatched, my boy,' Stephen warned Russ but at the thought of grandchildren his eyes shone with a new-found pride in his family.

Naturally enough, Brent turned to the decanters and passed drinks all round and the health and happiness of the newly engaged couple was a frequent toast during the next half hour.

Brent engaged to walk home with Sally and with great reluctance she and Russ parted from each other – but only until the following day as he pointed out to her. They had discussed plans for their wedding and everyone agreed that it should take place as quickly and as quietly as possible. Brent said lightly: 'I'd suggest that we make it a double wedding but I think Nancy wants to be the centre of attraction for one day, at least. In the future, she'll be shadowed completely by the limelight that falls on me – but I keep telling her that it's not my fault I'm a Power!'

Amid general laughter, the party broke up. Russ remained behind to talk to his father, Brent and Sally set off for her home and Matt discreetly withdrew from the room. He walked a few yards with Brent and Sally and then watched them as they continued on their way. He took out cigarettes and stood in the moonlight, smoking and very thoughtful.

After a while, he wandered about the gardens and before long he came upon the very hedge-lined avenue wherein he had first tried to kiss Promise and suffered for it! His lips twisted in the travesty of a smile – but he found no amusement in recalling that incident. Again and again, during the evening, his thoughts had turned to her – and reluctantly he was compelled to admit the truth that he had fallen deeply and irrevocably in love with Promise Power on that very evening when she had repulsed him so violently. It was grimly ironical that he had chosen to love the one woman in the world who detested him beyond measure.

Stephen Power's sons might be finding satisfaction in their various approaches to matrimony – but Matt Nellin, loved and trusted employee of the wealthy man, could find no satisfaction in the contemplation of his love for Stephen's daughter. The very thought that she might one day be persuaded to view him in a more friendly light caused him to burst into mocking laughter – laughter that mocked his own futile hopes and the very foolishness of his love for Promise. Sweet Promise. Again he laughed. She might be many things but sweet she certainly was not. He knew this was her frequently-bandied nickname among her friends and family. He even recalled Stephen Power's words to him, long before he met Promise: 'If you ever happen to meet my daughter, my sweet Promise, don't let her fool you! She's as cunning as they come and her tongue can match her temper at times. But for all that she's a lovable minx.'

She was indeed, Matt told himself bitterly. He had fallen in love without the slightest encouragement and despite his struggles to refute the truth. He recalled their violent altercations – and against his will he was forced to remember too the day when he had kissed her outside the offices of the Power Construction Company. The look in her eyes that day could never be forgotten and it was sufficient to impress upon him that any chance of his love finding response had died at birth!

No matter how difficult it might prove to carry out, he made a firm resolution that he would never again accept any invitation offered by Stephen Power which might involve a meeting with his daughter. If he did not meet Promise, if he firmly shut her out of his thoughts and closed his eyes, physically and mentally, to the memory of her disturbing loveliness, surely in time the image of her would dim and he would discover that he had nothing left of his love but cold ashes. At least he could hope!

There were other women in the world. He had no need to do as Jonothan had done – seek balm for his disappointment in religion and the monastic life. He was not doomed to a lonely existence for the rest of his life. Inevitably he must forget Promise and the love which burned so fiercely now and one day he would find himself in the throes of an aching, desperate need for another woman.

He strolled back to the house. Glancing through the drawing-room windows, he saw Russ and Stephen Power deep in discussion, many sheets of paper lying around them and several of the books which had engrossed Russ for weeks open and well-thumbed. He decided not to disturb them and entered the house through the library windows. He crossed the hall and began to mount the staircase. The telephone emitted its shrill summons and he paused. He waited a moment but no one came to answer it and he hurried back down the stairs and crossed to the telephone.

Promise's voice fell on his ears, breathless and faintly frightened. 'Oh, is that you, Matt! I'm glad it's you! I'm at the crossroads just beyond Mellingham. Would you take one of the cars and come here for me, Matt? It's important. Please come, Matt!'

It was so unusual for Promise Power to plead with anyone and her voice rang with so much urgency that he did not hesitate. 'I'll be there as quickly as I can. Are you all right?'

'Yes, of course. But please hurry!' She rang off and he replaced the receiver, a frown creasing his brow.

Something had evidently happened. It sounded very much as if she was stranded. He could well believe that she might have quarrelled with Tyler Bradford and he had driven away in fury, leaving her to make her own way home as best as she could.

He did not pause to find out if it was in order for him to borrow one of the cars. He hurried from the house and went round to the garages.

Within a few moments, he was hurtling down the drive in Promise's own white sports car, only a vague idea of the situation of the crossroads or Mellingham but determined to find them without waste of time...

CHAPTER FOURTEEN

Her dress lifted by the cool evening breeze, Promise hurried from the house with a smile for Ty who leaned across to open the car door.

'Hallo, sweet.' He bestowed a brief kiss on her cheek. 'You look like the promise of spring or some such thing.'

'Thank you,' she returned prettily.

They turned into the long drive and headed for the gates. 'I've reserved a table at the *Bull and Star*,' he said easily.

'It's a popular place, you know. I had some difficulty but fortunately the name of Bradford is just as influential as Power.' He grinned.

She looked at him, noticing for the first time his appalling air of conceit. She wondered briefly why she had always accepted it in the past and appreciated his pride in his family name. But this evening it jarred on her and she wondered if it was possible that her own pride and calm assumption that her name would work wonders had its own jarring effect on others. It wasn't possible that she was believed to be as unbearably conceited as Tyler Bradford!

He continued to chatter aimlessly during the drive but she returned monosyllables and made no attempt to stem the flow. He glanced at her curiously. 'You're very quiet this evening. Anything wrong?'

She forced a smile. 'Sorry. I was thinking about a man my father has invited for the week-end.'

His brows lowered ominously. 'That's bad policy.'

'What is, Ty?'

'Thinking of another man when you're with me. I call it the height of bad manners!' He spoke lightly enough but it was easy to detect his annoyance.

Promise laughed. 'You needn't worry, Ty. I can't stand him. He's the most insufferable, arrogant devil I've ever met.' But how more interesting than you, she suddenly thought – and was shocked by her own treachery.

'That's better.' He turned his head to smile at her and his eyes gleamed warmly as he looked at her, sitting so demurely in her yellow dress – and he had always believed that redheads shouldn't wear yellow: Promise certainly belied that fallacy – with her old-fashioned hair style and that tempting little body beneath the flimsy chiffon. The very tilt of her small nose excited him as did the wide, full mouth with its sensual underlip and the occasional hint of devilry in her wide-spaced grey eyes. He felt his heart pound and he determined that this evening he should know the full extent of her sweet desirability. He had waited long enough – and heaven knew he was never a patient man at the best of times.

Unaware of his thoughts, she gazed serenely at the passing countryside and tried not to think of the enjoyment she would have known if she had stayed at home that evening and baited Matt Nellin. She was growing bored with Ty. Strange that at one time she should have believed him to be the epitome of all she most admired in a man. During these last weeks, often in his company, she had come to know him thoroughly – his empty, superficial conversation, his never-failing good humour, his conceit and the obvious interest in women which he could not conceal even when they were together, his enjoyment of kisses that faintly repelled her and his restless hands which offended her sense of dignity, his lack of reserve and self-respect which she demanded in a man and, most of all, his disgusting failure to hold his drink. Yet she continued to go out with him because there was a faint excitement in being with a man she did not really like or trust – and also, though she would not admit it, because she knew that her father was a talkative man and suffered from an excess of prideful possessiveness where his family was concerned: Matt was certain to hear of her frequent appointments with Ty and deep in her heart she hoped that he would know a little jealousy – not much but enough to make him wish that he had not fallen foul of her so that he might be in Ty's place!

Ty did not like to drive too fast along the narrow lanes, much to Promise's contempt for she had always been used to speeding herself and revelling in her brother's skilful manoeuvres of the narrow lanes at high speed, and it was some time before they reached the roadhouse a few miles beyond Mellingham.

He drew into the forecourt and turned off the ignition. Then he turned to Promise. 'Kiss me before we go in,' he demanded. 'I shall have to share you with a great many people for the next few hours when I'd rather be alone with you – so give me one kiss to sustain me!' His arm about her shoulders he drew her to him and sought her mouth.

She submitted to the embrace, fighting against an instinctive revulsion as his mouth closed passionately upon her own. For perhaps the hundredth time she told herself that this was the last time she would go out with him as she pulled away and put her hands up to her hair.

'That's enough. You'll ruin my lipstick,' she protested as he would have kissed her again.

Inflamed by that first kiss, he was determined to have another and he said quietly: 'Damn your lipstick! Kiss me like a good girl!'

She opened the car door resolutely, brushing aside his restraining arm. 'I'm not a good girl – and the sooner you realise that the better we'll get on, Ty. Now behave yourself and let's eat. I'm hungry.'

He chuckled at her words and an angry flush stained her cheeks as she realised the meaning he had put to them. She stalked into the crowded, well-lit roadhouse with its garish decorations which she immediately disliked. Grimly she told herself that this was one evening she would be glad to forget swiftly.

But, to her surprise, she enjoyed the hours spent in the roadhouse. As though repentent for his roughness, Ty was the best of companions and she could find nothing objectionable in his manner or speech. By the time each had consumed a few drinks she was positively mellow towards him and wondered why she had ever thought that she disliked him. He was certainly handsome and she liked the way his eyes smiled when his lips curved into a smile. She liked his quiet, well-modulated voice and there seemed nothing inane or empty in his conversation this evening. She liked the firm, reassuring clasp of his hand and the smooth, easy way that he danced to the soft music of the orchestra. She liked his hard, powerful body so close to her own as she moved about the small floor in his arms. She liked the murmured endearments in her ear and the soft brushing of his lips against her hair.

They saw several mutual friends and it was almost instinctive to gravitate towards them – and before long they were a group of cheerful, slightly-intoxicated people and Promise laughed and talked and drank and was grateful to Ty for bringing her to the place and giving her such an enjoyable evening.

Towards the end of the evening, dancing with Ty, she felt his arm tighten about her waist and she glanced up just as he bent his head to kiss her lips. No one took any notice. There were too many couples openly embracing on the dance floor or at the tables or in quiet corners. Her lips parted slightly and she returned his kiss with easy fervour, knowing that she stirred him to passion and exulting in her never-failing power. It did not occur to her that it might be dangerous to excite a man already inflamed by drink and her proximity. She would have laughed if anyone had cautioned her, convinced of her ability to handle any man no matter what the situation. She did not mind that he held her so close. It was stimulating to feel the heavy pounding of his heart against her soft breast and she thought with real pleasure of the moment when she would repulse him firmly when he tried to take matters further, as she knew that he would.

At last, reluctantly, they left the roadhouse. Several minutes were spent in talking animatedly with their friends in the forecourt but Ty, impatient, finally pulled her away and led her towards his car. He closed the door firmly and went round to the driving seat. Driving away from the roadhouse, Promise turned in her seat to catch the last glimpses of their friends as their cars turned in a different direction.

Suddenly she spun round. 'This isn't the way to your home, Ty.'

He smiled at her. 'I know. But it's early yet, my sweet. I thought we'd have a moonlit drive through the countryside. I know a perfect place with a lake – secluded and quiet and really beautiful beneath the moon.'

She relaxed in her seat, lulled by his words and content to go wherever he decided to take her. She laughed softly and shook her head to clear it. 'I feel decidedly muzzy,' she said. 'Fresh air is exactly what I need.'

'That's what I thought,' he told her, well-pleased by her admission that the amount of alcohol she had taken was enough to dull her natural caution and yet stimulate her senses. He had been careful not to drink too much himself, knowing his own limitations in that direction, but had frequently refilled her glass. He smiled to himself as he drove on, confident that she would be unable to resist his advances even if she knew the desire to do so. He had been encouraged by her response to his kisses on the dance-floor and the warmest words and glances he had yet known from Promise. As he had suspected, there were exciting depths to her nature and a wealth of passion which he would take the greatest delight in arousing.

He turned into the narrowest of lanes off the main, only just wide enough to take his car, drove down it for some two hundred yards – and then drove out into a clearing with a lake that shimmered and sparkled in the moonlight.

Promise sat up abruptly, catching her breath. 'Oh, how lovely, Ty! Why haven't I ever been here before?'

'Not many people know of this place,' he told her, switching off the ignition and dropping the key into his pocket.

'I wish I'd brought a swimsuit with me,' she said ruefully. 'A moonlight swim would be really welcome just now.'

He smiled. 'I told you to pack one,' he said lightly.

She clapped her hands with sheer delight. 'Oh, of course. There's one in my case. Oh, Ty, do you think we could?'

'You can by all means but I haven't a spare

pair of bathing trunks in the dashboard, unfortunately.'

She pushed open the door and stepped out on to the springy turf. 'I don't think I can resist it,' she murmured as Ty came around the car to join her. He slipped his arm about her waist and drew her against him. She rested her head on his shoulder, a lovely smile touching her lips with a gentle curve, her eyes bright and eager.

'We're in no hurry,' he told her. 'You can change in the car. I'll walk to the edge of the lake and have a quiet cigarette.'

It did not take her long to rummage through her case, which Estelle had packed so neatly, bring out the swimsuit and strip off the flimsy dress and few brief under-things she wore. She wriggled into the swimsuit, a skin tight one-piece of black satin which clung delightfully to her youthful figure. Her feet bare she ran across the thick grass to join Ty who turned at her approach and eyed her with blatant admiration and a glimmering of desire – hastily she moved away from him and dipped one foot into the water.

'Brr! It's cold – but delicious!' she cried. She waded further into the water, watched by Ty who could scarcely control the flood of passion which swept over him. She was a strong and graceful swimmer and he watched as she streaked across the lake to the far side and then executed a neat turn and made her way back to him, more slowly. She trod water and waved to him. 'You don't know what you're missing,' she called. 'We must make up a party one night and come here for a midnight bathe again. It's great fun!'

He threw his cigarette to the ground and ground it firmly into shreds with his heel. 'That's enough,' he said authoritatively. 'I don't want you to catch cold, Promise.'

Reluctantly she waded out of the lake and he enveloped her slight body in the thick towel she had pulled from her case and given to him to hold while she swam. He rubbed her vigorously and she squirmed and wriggled, laughing as his firm fingers dug into her ribs.

'Is your hair wet?'

She touched it with her hands carefully. 'A little damp but don't worry about it, Ty. I don't want to spoil Estelle's handiwork just yet,' she told him lightly.

He longed to catch her close but her wet swimsuit made such a desire an impossibility. He caught his breath sharply as she pranced about on the grass, laughing at him gaily. Suddenly she darted towards the car. 'I'm going to dress. You stay there, Ty!'

It was the work of a few moments to change – but she found it more difficult to wriggle out of the wet suit than it had been to slip into it. She rubbed her body dry and hastily slipped on her clothes. She was glowing and her skin tingled with exhilaration, her cheeks flushed and her heart still racing from the exertion. When she was dressed she walked slowly back to Ty and accepted the cigarette which he offered. They stood in silence, faint wreaths of blue-grey mist rising above their heads to vanish into nothingness as it was caught and dispersed by the soft summer breeze.

Suddenly Promise shivered – and he turned to her swiftly. 'Cold?'

She shook her head. 'A goose walked on my grave,' she laughed.

He put his arm about her and she turned towards him, raising her face and eager for his embrace. He bent his head and kissed her, gently at first but gradually with urgency and he knew that she felt swift response to his own passion which betrayed itself by the hunger of his lips and the violence of his grip on her shoulder.

Still unafraid of him, it amused her to kiss him with still more warmth and to press her slim body against him ardently. When his hand strayed to the curve of her breast she made no objection but sighed deeply and nestled even closer to him.

As his kisses became more and more demanding, Promise knew a surge of panic but hastily she assured herself that she was perfectly safe if she kept cool and laughed off his passion – a technique that had worked admirably in the past. She drew away from him. 'Time we were moving on, Ty,' she said levelly.

Impatiently he took her arm and they walked to the parked car. She slid into her seat and he walked around to climb into his own seat. He turned on the small radio fitted into the dashboard and fiddled with it until he found a station that supplied soft, romantic music which suited the mood of the moment. He made no effort to start the car and Promise, her attention caught by a familiar tune, did not urge him to do so, intent upon following the lyrics with her own husky, rich singing voice. Unnoticed, Ty flicked a tiny switch which automatically locked the car doors, a little innovation of his own which few people knew or expected.

He relaxed comfortably and put his arm about her shoulders. 'Sleepy?'

She shook her head – and then as an enormous yawn took her by surprise and interrupted her rendering of the song, she laughed. 'Perhaps I am – a little. Swimming usually makes me sleepy – deliciously drowsy, anyway.'

'Rest your head on my shoulder,' he suggested and she did so willingly. He was careful not to rush his fences. So she lay against him and he contented himself for the time being with an occasional kiss on her hair and a gentle caressing of her bare, silky shoulder. She tilted her face to smile up at him and he recognised the look in her eyes as encouragement. He caught her close and kissed her hungrily, searchingly – and then Promise's hands flew to his hard chest in a scared effort to push him away.

But Ty had fed his imagination too well with the thoughts of such an opportune moment and desire had burned too frequently during the past weeks for him to accept that swift, angry denial. Inflamed and made furious by her apparent coquetry, he pulled her to him violently, crushing her in his strong arms, and buried his lips against the curve of her breast, murmuring passionate words so incoherently that she could only know a sense of shock and outraged modesty. If Matt could have witnessed her vehement outburst and her struggles to thrust Ty away from her, he would never again have believed her to be immoral, abandoned or easily flattered by male proximity.

The flimsy material of her dress was ripped as she struggled with him and his face bled from the sharp assault of her fingernails. Her hair tumbled from its neat bands and fell about her and she was glad of the thick, heavy tresses to conceal all that her ripped gown revealed.

Sobbing with panic and distress, she gained enough time to try the door but found to her horror that it was locked. She threw Ty such a reproachful, stricken look that he was instantly shamed and he released her abruptly, sat bolt upright in his seat and endeavoured to smooth his blond hair.

'You damned vixen!' he muttered but there was a trace of admiration in his voice for her spirit. He tasted blood on his lips from his scratched face and he was violently angry – but it was nothing compared to the tumult of fury that swept through Promise.

'How dare you! Take me home at once!'

she commanded furiously.

'Hell! You've been leading me on all night. What did you expect? Damn you, Promise! You've fooled me for weeks and now I find I've been wasting my time.'

'If I'd known that your only interest in me was so despicable, I would have told you immediately that you were wasting your time,' she told him in tones so icy that they immediately cooled any remaining desire. 'Take me home!'

'I'm damned if I will. My family expect you for the week-end,' he reminded her coldly.

'That's too bad! I've no intention of spending this week-end or any other with you and your family. If you're lost for an explanation, I'll gladly telephone your father and give him my reasons. In the meantime, please convey my apologies for the inconvenience – and drive me to my own home,' she said haughtily.

'Sorry,' he said bluntly. 'It's miles out of my way and it's late. If you must play the fool then you'll have to suffer for it. I shall enjoy the thought of your fifteen mile walk in that dress.' He unlocked the doors and threw open the one nearest to her. 'Out you get, you little tramp! Men have worse names than that for a girl like you – encouraging me for weeks and then putting on the old-fashioned outrage act!'

Thankfully she tumbled out of the car, unconcerned that she was a long way from home and only too glad that she could escape from Ty with nothing worse than a torn dress to commemorate the evening. He heaved her case out on to the grass then, with a sneering smile and a malicious wave of his hand, he drove off with a roar.

Promise stood irresolute for a moment, trembling all over, her face buried in her hands as tears of shock welled and overflowed. Then, struggling for composure, she walked to the lake, indifferent now to its beauty, and bathed her face and hands in the cool water, throwing her long dishevelled hair back over her shoulders. She dried herself with the skirt of her dress, desperately attempted to pin up her hair without success and ruefully regarded the scratches on her arms and shoulders and the curve of her breast. She was filled with acute loathing and contempt for Tyler Bradford but she dismissed him from her thoughts with the firm resolution to persuade Brent to teach him a lesson and a swift disappointment that she did not have enough courage to face the humiliation of a court case with all it would entail. For everyone in the county and beyond to know of the devilish situation in which she had placed herself and her panic-stricken struggles to ward off Ty's intentions would be more than she could bear.

She hurried along the dark lane, too much of a country girl to care for the threatening, sombre hedges or the possibility of coming across a stray animal or a tramp. She told herself grimly that indeed she would welcome the sight of a tramp who might be able to advise her as to short cuts back to her home. She had lost one of her evening sandals in the car and now she carried the other to make her progress easier. She stumbled in and out of potholes, hampered by the case which was heavier than she had imagined, wondering how on earth the car had traversed the miserable lane without coming to grief.

Reaching the main road, she saw and recognised the crossroads fifty yards away and she hastened towards the junction, remembering that there was a telephone box on the corner. She would telephone home and be sure of finding someone who had not yet gone to bed and who would be only too glad to drive out to pick her up...

CHAPTER FIFTEEN

Promise waited impatiently, cold and tired and still feeling the effects of the astonishing and hateful end to her evening with Ty. Every time a car approached she leaped up from the uncomfortable wooden seat thoughtfully provided by the Borough Council. Rushing to the edge of the grass verge, she hopefully scanned the oncoming car and its driver. Few cars were about at that time of night and none of the drivers bothered to give more than a passing glance to the slight, dishevelled figure at the side of the road.

She smoked interminably, wondering if Matt would find the crossroads without much difficulty, now fearful that he would fail her, then dreading his arrival and the inevitable questions.

She did not analyse her own relief at hearing his voice on the telephone rather than that of her father or one of her brothers. It had been so wonderful to hear a familiar, friendly voice and to know that within the space of an hour she would be safely in a car and on her way home. She knew that Matt would lose no time in reaching her. She could imagine his astonishment at her appeal and his swift determination to be with her as quickly as possible. For all his faults, he had a quick intelligence and a reliable streak in his character...

Matt was not very sure of his route but, by following signposts, he easily found Mellingham and it was the work of a few moments to pause at a garage and question the attendant about the location of the crossroads. To his relief, he found it was not only the junction of four main roads but also a well-known local district with a public house on the corner which was known as the *Crossroads Inn*.

He slowed as he neared the junction and saw Promise rush forward to the side of the road, hailing him with her hand. He braked with a long, protesting squeal from the tyres and clambered out swiftly, shocked and dismayed by her distressed appearance.

'What in hell...? Bradford, of course,' he said grimly and knew a rush of icy anger.

So relieved to see him, she suddenly began to cry soundlessly, the tears streaming down her flushed cheeks and glistening in the moonlight which turned night almost into day. He took her by the shoulders and kissed her cheek tenderly. 'Don't cry, Promise. You're safe now.'

She clung to him, sobs shaking her slight body and he held her close, soothing her with gentle words. 'He was horrible...' she sobbed. 'Beast – foul-minded beast!'

'You're safe now,' he assured her again. 'I'll drive you home and when you've had a drink and a hot bath, you'll feel much better.'

She was so startled by his unexpected kindness and concern, such a contrast to Ty's rough inconsideration, that her tears were abruptly stemmed. She drew away from him, conscious now of her embarrassing gratitude for the security and reassurance of his arms, knuckling her eyes in a childlike gesture. 'I'm all right now, Matt,' she said slowly. 'I'm sorry. Silly of me to break down but – it was so hateful...' Her voice trailed off thinly.

'Try to forget it,' he told her, tilting her chin with a gentle finger. 'But I promise you that he won't get away with it... I shall make it a personal challenge to settle your score with Tyler Bradford,' he added grimly.

She looked at him quickly but decided to make no reply. She moved towards the car. 'My case is on that seat,' she said. 'Could you heave it into the back, Matt?'

He did as she requested without comment, walked around to the driving seat and slipped in beside her. She said abruptly: 'Matt, there's some brandy in the dashboard by your hand. I always keep it there in case of emergency!'

'Sensible girl!' He approved. 'Just the thing you need right now.' He handed the flask, first unscrewing and removing the cap, but he watched her carefully and took the flask from her hand when he decided that she had sipped enough of the fiery liquid. 'Feel better?'

She nodded. 'Much better, thanks.'

He stripped off his jacket and passed it across to her. 'Here – put this on. It's not a very warm night.'

She huddled into the coat, grateful for his swift thought, aware that he was more concerned for the embarrassing condition of her once-lovely gown than for the chill of the night air. Apart from that first, startled dismay, he had been completely at ease and she had almost forgotten her appearance in the comfort of his presence and the knowledge that she would soon be home again.

He seemed in no hurry to start the car and she glanced at him curiously. He sensed her gaze and he turned to look at her anxiously. 'I don't want to embarrass you, Promise, but I must know. Are you sure you're all right?'

She immediately understood and she smiled at him with cheerful reassurance. 'Of course. I can fight like that wildcat you once compared me with. Ty will have some trouble explaining away the state of his face,' she added with loathing in her voice.

'Thank heavens for that, anyway!' he muttered and putting his arm about her shoulders he gave her a brief hug. She stared at him in amazement for she would never have believed that he could ever show affection or such concern for her well-being. She noticed the set of his lips, the resolute jut of his jawline, and she was touched by his evident anger against Ty. Complacently she told herself that once Matt had summarily dealt with the man she need never fear his attentions again. Although it was most unlikely that Ty would have any further interest in her for she sensed that he was not accustomed to rebuffs. She would not have been so surprised if Matt had told her coldly that she had laid herself wide open for the insult handed out by Ty. But there had been no reproaches. He had been kind, considerate and swiftly understanding and there had been no awkwardly embarrassing questions. He had obviously taken in the situation at a glance. For the first time she realised that she had misjudged Matt Nellin. He was not the cruel and ruthless rogue that she had believed him to be. She would have been safer in his company that night despite his rapid approach on their first meeting. At least he would have respect for her – and it was the most galling realisation of all that Ty did not respect any woman who led him to believe that his advances would be welcome. She knew that she was greatly to blame. She had encouraged Ty during the weeks of their friendship and, most of all, during that evening, a little light-headed because of the amount she had drunk at the *Bull and Star* and finding him oddly attractive and likeable in violent contrast to her earlier distaste and dislike.

She wished now that she had never taken up with Ty but she had not heard anything detrimental about his character in the past and she had taken his clean, fresh looks at face value.

Matt started the car and turned in the road so that they faced the homeward path. After a few moments, he replaced his arm about her shoulders and she relaxed against him, weary and sick at heart.

During the drive, he told her of his walk with Brent to the *Crooked Scythe*, his persuasion of Sally to walk in on Russ without warning, the success of the idea and she listened eagerly, delighted to hear that the affair had finally reached a satisfactory conclusion. She said as much and he raised an eyebrow cynically.

'I thought you were against the idea of having Sally Whitlock for a sister-in-law?'

She smiled. 'I've no right to object to my brother's wish to marry Sally,' she conceded honestly. 'I've nothing against the girl personally. Anyway, even if I had, I'd keep quiet if Russ is happy about it. I've hated to see him looking so unhappy and strained – and I'm not so insensitive that I've believed it was all due to his accident.'

'I hope you've forgiven me for my part in that,' he said quietly.

Promise shrugged. 'Oh, I expect the same thing would have happened eventually. Russ

258

was always a dare-devil but he's changed so much now.'

He grinned. 'Apparently you're not pleased about that?'

'Yes, I am,' she affirmed stoutly. 'It was good fun in the old days when the boys were always thinking up some new prank. But they took a long time to mature. I've sometimes thought lately that they were too old for such high spirits – that it was time they took life more seriously.'

'But it doesn't apply to you?'

She moved impatiently in her seat. 'Yes, it does.'

He looked at her curiously. 'You're not a very happy person, are you, Promise?'

She laughed. 'What a ridiculous idea! Of course I'm happy, Matt. I have everything to ensure happiness. Why on earth should you make such a statement?'

'I guess it's just an impression,' he said slowly. 'It strikes me that a girl like you wouldn't bother with Tyler Bradford if you weren't bored and restless and looking for kicks. Sometimes I've wondered if you're envious because all your brothers seem to be finding their particular brand of happiness – even if you don't approve of their choice. Believe me, Promise, you needn't worry that you'll be left on the shelf!'

She stiffened. 'I'm not anxious to marry,' she said coldly. 'As for being left on the shelf, that's most unlikely – even if I'm married for my money,' she added bitterly.

'I should imagine that any man would be glad to marry you even if you're a poor man's daughter,' Matt said quietly.

She laughed. 'Well, that's encouraging. Thank you for the compliment – the first I've had from you, I believe.'

'The first of many, perhaps.'

'Why? Are you changing your mind about me?' she teased. 'Have you suddenly discovered that I'm not such a detestable shrew as you thought?'

He did not smile. 'Your opinion of me has never been any more complimentary,' he reminded her.

'That's your fault!' she said sharply. 'You've always been most objectionable to me – insulting and humiliating me as often as you could. You can't expect to be popular with that technique!'

'I wasn't going all out for your liking,' he retorted. 'Is it surprising that I was not impressed with you when your father did his utmost to laud your praises without ceasing

260

from the first day of employing me?'

She frowned. 'I know what you mean. Father does overdo it. But you can't blame him for being proud and fond of me!'

'If I were your father I wouldn't be very proud of you,' he returned. 'You've been a handful since you were learning to walk – or so he tells me! As much trouble as your brothers – and they've caused plenty, I gather.'

She flushed. 'Look here, I'm grateful to you for saving me a long walk home. But not grateful enough to listen to your criticisms without protest! I'd say that your own life has been pretty wild, judging by the stories you told my father and brothers, so you needn't hide behind smug sanctity and lay down the law to me!'

'Okay, so I've been pretty wild. But I don't think anyone has ever suffered through me! To my recollection, I've never seduced another man's fiancée or broken anyone's jaw or busted up a bar in a fight. When I have to fight then I do – but never for the hell of it! I've more respect for the conventions than you might think!'

'How exceedingly dull,' she said lightly.

'Maybe,' he returned curtly.

They sat in affronted silence for a few

minutes, Matt pointedly removing his arm to drive with both hands on the steering wheel. She missed its comforting presence but set her jaw firmly and stubbornly. It was nothing to her that he was once more angry with her and that their hope of forming a friendship to replace the previous hostility had crumpled abruptly with the hard words. She sat stiffly beside him, ignoring him.

It seemed incredible that she had been blind to the evil in Ty's nature until he had shown his true colours that night. She had been a fool to ignore her instinctive revulsion and snatch at the dangerous excitement of going out with a man whom she could not wholly trust. She should have followed her inner hesitation from the beginning and realised that Ty was not a man noted for his morals, his integrity or his consideration. She could not imagine any other man turning her from his car to make her way home as best as she could with fifteen miles to cover. Oh, he was hateful and despicable and she would never speak to him again...

She had been markedly unfortunate in her choice of men-friends throughout the years. Several times she had believed herself in love only to discover the shallowness of her emotion when she learned that the man in question was more interested in her father's money than in herself. She had been successful in dismissing the men from her thoughts and from her life without difficulty and turned with warm eagerness towards a newcomer with the hope that this time she would inspire a real, sincere and dis-interested love. Or she had found herself completely unable to respond to the emotion she evoked in others and regretfully broken off the association as it became obvious that a proposal of marriage was imminent.

She was twenty-three and unmarried. It was no great age but as she noted the successful and happy love affairs of the girls in her social circle who were about her age, it seemed that she was doomed to spinster-hood. A ridiculous fancy, as she frequently told herself, but she had never yet found a man who compared favourably with her ideal or to whom she could willingly give her heart. A true woman, she sometimes hankered for a man's love, a home of her own, children to bring happiness to her marriage – and the undeniably envied status of being a wife.

Her humiliating experience with Ty had its

reaction in a dismayed thought that she might always find that men had only two intentions where she was concerned – either to marry her for the sake of her father's money or to seduce her without a thought for marriage. She shrank from this thought and assured herself emphatically that one day she would be fortunate enough to find love and happiness with a man worthy of her heart.

Matt glanced covertly at her, his own thoughts busy. He had not intended to quarrel with her again and he was grieved that his tongue had run away with him. He longed to stop the car, put his arms about her and convince her with his kisses that she was the only woman in the world for him, despite everything that had happened since their first meeting. But he controlled the impulse, miserably certain that she would repulse him without hesitation and throw icy scorn on his hopes and aspirations. Now he understood why he had felt uneasy during the evening. His thoughts had been mainly with Promise and he had disliked the knowledge that she was enjoying herself with another man. On the few occasions that he had seen Tyler Bradford with Promise, he had been unimpressed by his looks or personality and he had been swift to disapprove of her taste in escorts. Perhaps he had sensed that Bradford was not to be trusted. But the fact that he had been uneasy could not be denied and during his fast drive across country he had been convinced of the truth behind her unexpected and appealing telephone call. His anger against Bradford had been aroused long before he saw her badly-torn dress, the scratches on her arms and breast and her hair flowing wildly about her bare shoulders. Holding her while she cried against his chest, he had known a violent wish to settle the matter with Bradford without mercy or consideration.

He looked at her again and this time their eyes met. Briefly, coldly, their gaze held – and then she smiled. 'Don't look so grim, Matt.'

His expression softened at the warmth in her voice. 'Sorry. I was thinking of Bradford!'

'Well, that's a relief!' she told him lightly. 'I really thought I'd brought that look to your eyes. I know how much you dislike me but I didn't think you'd make it quite so obvious.'

'I don't dislike you,' he replied tensely.

She put her hand on his arm and squeezed

it gently. 'If you were to say that less violently I might believe you.'

'You wouldn't believe it, anyway,' he retorted. 'I've said too many hard things in the past to convince you now that most of them were said in anger and shouldn't be taken seriously.'

She smiled up at him. 'Things said in anger are invariably the truth, Matt. Who bothers with politeness or tact or consideration for another person's feelings when they are angry? I haven't any doubt that you dislike me intensely and think I'm a stupid little fool old enough to know better. That's all right with me, though. I'd much rather be sincerely disliked by a man like you than suffer your indifference!'

'What a strange woman you are!' he blurted in astonishment.

'Not really. I think most women would feel the same way. Indifference can be very hurtful. Dislike only puts me on my mettle and makes me either determined to convince the person who dislikes me that I'm everything they believe me to be – or else determined to win them over at all costs so that one day they admit that they were quite wrong about me!'

As he turned into the drive of her home

and began to mount the steep, winding curve of its beginning, he said without looking at her: 'Which heading do I come under?'

She lifted her hands to her heavy mass of auburn hair, raising it from her shoulders and throwing it back with a careless, lovely gesture. 'I'm not likely to tell you, now, am I? That would spoil everything!'

He made no reply and within a few moments they were at a standstill outside the big door of the house with its stone steps leading up to it.

She stepped from the car and walked around it. Then she put her hands on his shoulders and kissed him briefly on the lips – so briefly that it was barely a brushing of her mouth against his own. 'Thank you for coming to the rescue,' she said softly. 'I shall go straight to my room. Please don't tell anyone what happened. The whole thing is best forgotten.'

He raised an eyebrow. 'I don't agree with you.'

'Naturally you don't – but it is my business and my experience and I don't wish to share it with my family. Ty would be torn limb from limb if Brent knew what had happened tonight.'

'He'd have a willing accomplice in me,' Matt said swiftly, dangerously.

'I'd rather avert a scandal, just the same. It was quite humiliating enough without the whole world knowing the truth. So, if you don't mind, Matt – forget the whole thing!'

'Oh, sure!' he jeered. 'And let Bradford get away with it?'

She smiled sweetly. 'I know he won't, Matt. But surely you can handle him without Brent's help?'

He met her eyes levelly. 'Don't sweet-talk me, Promise.'

She turned away with a laugh and ran up the stairs, his jacket still about her shoulders. She paused on the top step and looked back. 'I'll leave your coat in your room,' she assured him.

He nodded and let in the clutch. She watched as he drove slowly around the house and disappeared out of sight, en route to the garages.

CHAPTER SIXTEEN

Matt did not see Promise again that night. When he returned to the house, Stephen came out of the library and strode towards him. 'So there you are at last. I wondered what had happened to you, Matt. Brent was back some time ago and looked blank when I asked where you were. I thought you'd decided to go with him and Sally.'

Lamely he offered an excuse about the beauty of the night and the appeal of a drive into the country. His employer's eyes narrowed. 'Without a coat, boy? That won't wash, you know!'

'Promise needed my coat,' he returned deliberately.

Stephen stared at him. 'Promise? What are you talking about, boy?'

Quietly, concisely, Matt explained – and watched Stephen Power's expression change from bewilderment to astonishment to anger. He strode to the foot of the stairs and bellowed his daughter's name.

Startled, Matt said hastily: 'I expect she's

in bed, Steve. Leave it till the morning.'

Stephen glared at him. 'I mean to get to the bottom of this tonight.' Again he bellowed for Promise and this time she appeared at the head of the stairs within a moment, enveloped in a dressing-gown, annoyance in her eyes.

'Be quiet, Father! Do you want to wake the household?'

'Come down here – and don't backtalk me!' he snapped.

With an audible sigh, she ran down the staircase and threw an accusing, reproachful glance at Matt who spread his hands in a helpless gesture.

'What is it, Father?' She turned to him impatiently.

'Matt has just told me an amazing story about you and Tyler Bradford. I'll have it from you now – with explicit details.'

'Father, it's over and done with. There isn't any point in holding a post-mortem at this time of night,' she reproached. 'Ty tried to get fresh. I made it very clear that he was wasting his time and he drove off in a huff, leaving me stranded. I telephoned Matt and he came to bring me home. That's all there is to it.'

His sharp eyes studied her. Suddenly he

wrenched open her dressing-gown and examined the scratches on her slim body. His face darkened. Promise wrenched away, furious and embarrassed, and drew the gown about her slim body which had been revealed in all its beauty by her father's swift movement. 'I'll have that fellow in court if it's the last thing I do,' Stephen said grimly.

'It won't do any good. Let it drop, Father,' she said angrily. 'If you think I'm going to get up in any court and tell the world what happened tonight, then you're mistaken. There's no harm done – except for a few scratches and Ty looks worse than I do.' She laughed humourlessly. 'I concentrated on his face. He won't be very keen to show himself for a few days.'

'He'll never set foot inside this house again. I don't care what you say, Promise. He isn't going to get away with this!'

Matt stepped forward. 'Go back to your room, Promise,' he said firmly. 'Now, Steve – come and have a drink and let's talk this over sensibly. You don't want to embarrass Promise, surely. It's been bad enough for her – and as she says, there isn't much point in dragging the whole affair through the courts. You seem to forget that Promise has been going out with him for some weeks

271

and he's bound to claim that she encouraged him and seemed a willing party but panicked at the last moment. Do you want the world to call your daughter a tramp – or worse?'

Realising that Matt had matters in hand, Promise slipped away and sped back to her room. She was remarkably grateful to him. She had known by the light in her father's eyes that he was determined to carry out his threat – but as she left the two men, she had recognised a hint of hesitation in his manner and she felt sure that Matt would win the day.

Dear Matt! Kind and thoughtful and wise. She had never believed the day would dawn when she would be thankful for his presence and relying on him to extricate her from an unpleasant experience.

She lighted a cigarette and walked over to the open window. The soft breeze ruffled the short, crisp strands which curled about her temples and small, shell-like ears. It disturbed the folds of her gown and caressed the velvety skin. It cooled her flushed face and brought a sparkle to her lovely eyes. She stared at the dark, velvety sky with the round, full moon which stared back at her unblinkingly.

Her thoughts turned to Matt's arms about her and the soft tenderness of his kiss on her cheek when he soothed her tears at the roadside. She had clung to him without reserve and found solace in his warm, hard proximity, the quiet murmured soothing of his voice, the integrity and reliability which she had instinctively sensed in his character. But they had argued again during the drive home – and she had been hurt and dismayed by his hard words. It was astonishing that he had the power to hurt her, to pierce her sensitivity, to goad her into taunts she neither meant or intended to say.

Would they always quarrel so bitterly? It was apparent that her father was devoted to Matt and therefore it was inevitable that she would see more and more of him as time passed.

It was odd but she was glad of this. For the first time she admitted to herself that she had been weak and responsive in his arms when he kissed her in the taxi on the day when they had lunched together. She had thrilled to his kiss, to the scarcely-concealed power of his embrace, to the hint of passion which had leaped to his dark eyes. She had tried again and again to forget that moment but it had been impossible and now it came back to her with intensified force. She tried to dismiss the disturbing realisation that she wanted to be kissed by him again – and to return his ardour without resentment and anger against him to mar the moment. She tried to ignore the sudden leap of her heart and the wild tumult of longing which swept through her entire being.

It was ridiculous! She moved impatiently and threw her cigarette through the open window. It soared in a wide arc and finally fell to the ground to scatter in a blaze of bright sparks. Matt Nellin was ruthless and despicable – but she was lying to herself and she abruptly rescinded the thought. Ruthless meant without mercy or consideration and that was not true of Matt. How could he be despicable when she had found him trustworthy and integral, kind and considerate and understanding, and had been moved by the touch of his lips and the security of his arms. Had she been lying to herself for weeks? Was it possible that she had thrown herself into an affair with Ty merely to still the tiny voice in her heart which cried in vain for the love of a man like Matt.

She heard firm footsteps pass her door and the leap of her heart assured her that it must be Matt on his way to his room. She flew to the door, wanting to speak to him, hoping for warmth in his eyes and on his tongue, unconcerned in that moment that he might leap to conclusions if she betrayed her eagerness and longing. But as she opened her bedroom door she heard the faint, final snap of his own door as he entered the room. Slowly, disappointed and suddenly depressed, she pushed the door closed and sank on to the side of her bed. He had no time for her. How often had he impressed that upon her. She was proud and wilful and arrogant, haughty and quarrelsome, cold and defiant and scornful. She should not expect him to have a very high opinion of her. She had thrown away every chance of winning his approval or his affection.

It seemed a bitter blow of Fate that she should have antagonised the one man whom she could have loved with all the passionate force of her being. From the very beginning she had torn down every flimsy attempt to win her friendship that he had put up. She had insulted and humiliated him, mocked and scorned him, quarrelled with him in bitter, furious animosity – and now she had the temerity to hope that there

275

might still be a chance to gain his liking and respect.

A low knock on her door caused her to jump with surprise. Hastily she went to the door and opened it. Matt nodded to her. 'I'm sorry, Promise. Were you in bed?'

She stared at him. 'No – not yet.'

'What did you do with my coat?' he asked quietly. 'My cigarettes are in the pocket.'

'Oh! I meant to take it to your room.' She turned from the door swiftly and picked up his coat from her bed. She smiled at him tentatively, shyly. 'Why don't you come in and share a cigarette with me, Matt?'

He looked at her swiftly, surprised! 'It's rather late, Promise. You should be thinking about sleep. Thanks all the same but I'll go to my own room.'

Her face clouded. 'As you wish,' she said shortly and handed his coat across to him.

'By the way, I talked your father out of a court case,' he said abruptly. 'I guess you've been anxious.'

'You did? Oh, thank heavens! I'm so grateful to you, Matt. The very thought of taking Ty to court was distasteful – and after all, it would only be my word against his!'

She was beautiful as she gazed up at him with eyes bright with relief, a smile trembling on her lips. Matt looked long and silently into her eyes – then abruptly, fearful of betraying himself, he turned to walk away.

Promise caught at his hand. 'Matt!'

He turned, surprised. 'Yes?'

'Please don't go yet. Stay and talk to me,' she pleaded.

She was trembling from head to foot and he could not give a name to the expression of her wide-set grey eyes. 'There's nothing to worry about now,' he said reassuringly. 'Get some sleep and in the morning you'll have forgotten it all.'

'Matt!' She said his name in anguish.

He stepped into the room, disturbed. 'Okay. One cigarette and then I'm definitely going to my own room.' He pulled the crumpled pack from his pocket and offered it to her. Promise took a cigarette and bent her head over the flame of his lighter. Straightening up, she walked away from him, fighting against the flood of emotion and a desperate shyness which was completely new to her.

'So Brent has arranged a busy week-end for you,' she said lightly, with a real effort to keep her voice steady. 'Riding and shooting and fishing. Do you like all those things?'

'Well enough. I was brought up in the country.'

She turned eagerly. 'I've never been to Canada. Do tell me about it, Matt! Is it very different to England? Why did you take up Dad's offer of a job to come over here? Will you go back to Canada one day?'

'Hey, hold on!' he said with a light laugh. 'Must I answer all those right now. It's a little late for a discourse on Canada, don't you think. There's plenty of time over the week-end for that.'

She moved her slim shoulders in a tiny shrug. 'Oh, Brent will monopolise you – or Father will. You won't want to spend your time telling me about Canada.' She spoke a little petulantly.

'I could find time for you if you wanted it that way,' he replied slowly, narrowing his eyes in bewilderment. Suddenly his gaze sharpened. 'I hope you're not planning to amuse yourself with me now that you're suddenly bereft of a boy-friend,' he said grimly. 'Because I'm not in the mood for a light flirtation right now, Promise.'

She flushed. She stubbed her cigarette and moved towards him. She put her arms about his neck and gazed into his eyes seriously. 'I'm not thinking of a light flirtation, Matt.'

He raised his hands to loosen her embrace. 'You're wasting your time!'

Pain stabbed her heart and she knew a strange, uncomfortable sickness at the pit of her stomach. 'Is that the truth, Matt?' she asked slowly, painfully. 'Is it so impossible for you to alter your opinion of me? Will you always hate me so much?'

'I don't hate you,' he said, moved to compassion by the look in her eyes and yet completely taken aback by her odd and abrupt change of attitude towards him.

She clenched her hands and turned her back to him so that he should not see the despair in her eyes or the trembling of her lower lip. 'Thanks,' she said flippantly. 'Very reassuring of you!'

'You puzzle me,' he said slowly.

'Do I?' Her voice was muffled.

'Is this another trick, Promise?' he demanded with some heat. 'You're not going to lead me up the garden path and then laugh in my face.'

She swung round. 'I wouldn't do that, Matt! I swear I wouldn't! Can't you see that I just wish we were friends? It's so pointless to be always at loggerheads.'

'Sorry,' he said lightly. 'Friendship is out of the question.' He did not add that it was too late for friendship between them, that he wanted her love or nothing, that if it was to be nothing then the best thing for him was to fade out of her life without further delay.

'I see,' she said stiffly. 'Well, it's my own fault, I suppose.' She ran her hand across her eyes swiftly. 'Finished your cigarette?' she asked lightly.

He stubbed it abruptly. 'If that's a polite way of telling me to get out, yes!'

'Are you always so sensitive?' she demanded hotly.

He grinned without warmth or humour. 'I guess you usually manage to hit a raw spot.'

She held out her hand to him. 'At least I can apologise for always being so rude to you. I'm sorry that you won't be friends with me but I can't blame you, Matt.'

He caught and held her fingers tightly. 'Don't misunderstand me, Promise,' he said urgently. 'If you'd asked for my friendship a few months ago I'd have been only too willing to give it. A few hard words are easily forgotten. But now – well, frankly, I couldn't swear to keep it on a strictly friendly basis!'

She stared at him in disbelief – and then eager, radiant incredulity. 'Matt?' There was a note of hope, an eager question, a swift, unmistakable inflection in the one word.

He caught her to him, forced her face upwards with unintentional violence and gazed deeply into her eyes. 'If you're playing a game of your own I'll make you suffer for it,' he told her harshly. 'I love you too much to be fooled with!'

She caught her breath. She had never hoped, even in the wildest moment, that he might already love her. She had humbly hoped only for his friendship as a beginning, almost afraid to be confident of eventually winning his affection. She could not believe that her ears had not deceived her.

But Matt did not give her time enough to ponder the matter. His lips sought hers hungrily and she closed her eyes as emotion flooded her and the fervent reassurance of his kiss was the only important thing in the world.

Against his lips, she murmured softly, happily: 'I do love you so, Matt. How silly of us both to waste so much time!'

He pulled away and laughed at her, his dark eyes teasing her. 'Wasted? Of course it wasn't. I've found out what a shrew of a wife I shall have to tame – and it's a good thing to be prepared!'

She laughed with him and retorted: 'And I've learned never to do anything to you that I wouldn't want done to me – like throwing things at you or slapping your face! You so quickly return the compliment!'

He hugged her and kissed her swiftly. 'My darling – I'll never willingly hurt or offend you again.'

'And I'll never quarrel with you again,' she promised – but they both knew that there would be many a hard word, many an obstacle brought about by their stubborn, wilful characters and quick tempers to be overcome, many moments when one or the other would be hurt or dismayed by a thoughtless word or action. Yet, secure in their love for each other, they had no fear of the future and each knew that only by sharing the years ahead could they hope for happiness in life – and as their lips met in the expression of their love, that kiss was a sweet promise of greater joy than either had ever known.

The publishers hope that this book has given you enjoyable reading. Large Print Books are especially designed to be as easy to see and hold as possible. If you wish a complete list of our books please ask at your local library or write directly to:

Dales Large Print Books
Magna House, Long Preston,
Skipton, North Yorkshire.
BD23 4ND

This Large Print Book, for people
who cannot read normal print,
is published under the auspices of

THE ULVERSCROFT FOUNDATION

Other DALES Titles
In Large Print

VICTOR CANNING
The Golden Salamander

HARRY COLE
Policeman's Prelude

ELLIOT CONWAY
The Killing Of El Lobo

SONIA DEANE
Illusion

ANTHONY GILBERT
Murder By Experts

ALANNA KNIGHT
In The Shadow Of The Minster

GEORGES SIMENON
Maigret And The Millionaires